# ASYLUM

## BY

## KEV KIRK

## AN SLK CONSTRUCTION

ALSO BY KEV KIRK

ADMISSION

This book is a work of fiction.

Any resemblance to people, living or dead, is purely coincidental.

However, the geography is real.

As far as I remember.

For my family.


And

Everyone whose job is about more than just paying bills.

*It may seem a strange principle to enunciate as the very first requirement in a hospital that it should do the sick no harm.*

**Florence Nightingale.**

An early advance in the pharmacological treatment of mental illness proved to be the discovery that the administration of emetics was of benefit in relieving some symptoms. After a prolonged period of induced vomiting the resulting exhaustion calmed those suffering with mania and other nervous disorders. The risk of the patient choking on inspired vomit was deemed worth the positive outcome of the treatment. As a measure of this treatments success it was noted that in many cases the patient's handwriting once again became legible.

…Things could only get better…

Surely?

ONE NIGHT, FIVE YEARS AGO.

Against the dark, cloud laden, late autumn sky St. Mark's hospital had become a silhouette. The steep, angular roofline pointed to the sky above dark windows and century old brickwork. A cold wind whispered passed the chimneys and around the corners of the building. Sudden gusts caused the occasional shriek, like voices calling from the past.

Mick Draper concluded his circuit of the exterior of the hospital and stood by the back entrance. The spotlight above the doors cast a pool of light around him and illuminated the cars parked in the gated compound. Beyond the metal fence the heavy machines belonging to the construction company caught the light. Beyond them all was darkness and silence.

Mick slipped his Maglite back into the holder on his utility belt as the glass doors closed behind him. He unzipped his black, padded jacket and automatically checked the mobile phone and bunch of keys attached to his belt were in place. He gave a soft grunt when he noticed that his highly polished boots had picked up some mud during his patrol. Turning away from the doors he started along the main rear corridor of the hospital.

Technically Mick's job title was Porter. However, at night that doubled as security. It was that aspect of the job he relished most. It appealed to his military aspirations. A few years with the TA had whetted his appetite for a military life, but the death of his father and the care of his mother had thwarted those ambitions. Still, Mick knew, on his watch the patients and staff of the hospital were in safe hands. He had read every book he could get his hands on about the SAS, unarmed combat and guerrilla tactics.

The long corridor, illuminated by fluorescent lighting, stretched ahead of him. To his left a few dark windows looked out onto the night. On his right, scattered along the hundred metres of the corridor, a few doors led to storage areas and long abandoned rooms, with windows shuttered, and in some cases painted over, on the inside. This side of the hospital was not a patient area. The main wards were to the front of the building. Those still in use as the gradual closure of the old edifice progressed.

The bland, vinyl floored corridor was cold and Mick's footsteps echoed around him as he marched smartly along. It was an area of the hospital that had a bad reputation at night time. People reported odd noises, fluctuations in temperature, some claiming to have seen shadowy figures that appeared and vanished through doors or around corners. One of his colleagues had once claimed his clip-on tie was snatched from his throat by invisible fingers and flung along the floor. Mick thought all that was nonsense, but still he made towards his exit at a good rate.

Mick's aim was the next right turn where the corridor was carpeted, warmer, and led towards the more populated area of the hospital. Twenty-five metres ahead, the junction was within reach when he was halted in his tracks by the thump of something hitting the wall beside him. He looked up and down the empty corridor. The noise had come from behind the wall to his right.

Mick took a few paces backwards and stood and looked at the scarred wooden surface of the door he had just passed. A window, a little further back, covered inside by what looked like a heavy blackout blind. Behind the door something fell with a soft thud and there was the sound of softer, rattling impacts as though something were being scattered across the floor. Mick pulled his Maglite from his belt. The long torch was not just bright, it was heavy and made an effective baton.

Mick looked up and down the corridor again. He thought briefly of Maureen, the night manager, with who he had a regular arrangement. The person he had been heading towards. He did not need some errant patient or bored member of staff interfering with his nights activities. The room behind the door was a storage facility. There was no reason for anyone to be in there on a night. So, what had just been kicked across the floor and hit the wall again as he stood there?

Mick pulled his key from his belt. The universal hospital door key came away from his hip, still attached to the fob on his belt by a cord. He reached out and tried the handle of the door and experienced the first real qualms about the situation. The metal was as cold as ice. Transferring the Maglite to his left hand he slipped the key into the lock, turned it then pushed the door open without stepping forward. The key, still attached to the fob, tugged at his belt. He pulled it from the lock.

"Someone in here?" Mick said loudly, remaining in the corridor. He turned the torch on and pointed it into the doorway. All that faced him was a cream wall a metre away. The entrance to the room was a dark aperture immediately to the right of the door.

Inside the dark room something slid across the floor.

"Hello?" Mick leant forward and groped inside the door for a light switch. He played the torchlight across the entrance to the room. The beam illuminated a pile of boxes. One was upset and the contents, what looked like spools of tape, strewn across the floor. "Security! You've no business being in here," he said. There was a slight catch in his voice that he regretted.

His fingers found the switch for the lights and flicked it. Nothing happened. Mick muttered a short curse and stepped towards the room entrance. He stood still and swung the beam of the light across the room. More boxes, stacked shoulder high in some places. More tapes on the floor. Some of them large thick spools with black tape. Video, before the arrival of cassettes, he realised. Against the wall, behind the boxes, were some antique glass fronted cabinets holding shelves of leather backed books. The room smelt damp, the air cold. The space seemed to bend away from him in a L shape, beyond the reach of his torch.

"Okay," Mick said to himself, "rats."

Something moved with a rustling sound to his left, beyond the corner of the room. Mick swung the beam of the Maglite towards the sound.

He tried to call out but his voice was a strangled croak in his constricted throat.

Mick swung around and jumped through the doorway back into the corridor almost before the crash of the dropped torch echoed around the room. He looked back at the open door once as he bolted for the junction and the carpeted corridor.

A bizarre thought popped into his head through the fear propelling him to escape.

There was nothing in the SAS manuals about keeping a spare pair of trousers in your kit.

2

Frank Blake rolled over on the bed and groaned. The crack in the ceiling plaster that looked like the profile of a demented clown smiled away, like everything was right with the world. She turned her head and glared at the clock on the bedside cabinet.

"Two-o-bloody-clock!" Kicking the duvet away she sat up and swung her legs over the side of the bed. She looked at the damning digits on the clock and thumped the pillow. "Four bloody hours sleep!"

Frank hated night shifts. Or, more accurately she hated her inability to sleep during the day. No matter how tired she felt at 3am, when her eyes were rolling and her mind drifting, come daylight her brain refused to acknowledge her exhaustion and nudged her awake after less sleep than an insomniac on speed.

"I need a new job," Frank announced and fell back onto the bed.

She gazed at the cracked plaster above her. The crack reminded her of Pete and his promise to fix it.

"Oh, and let's not even go there, thank you," Frank told herself. She did not need her mind turning over every dirty stone in the garden to add to how lousy she felt.

Catching her husband in the throes of passion had brought her five years of marriage to a bitter end. The memory of Peter Rudd's hands lifting the hem of that red leather miniskirt was etched on her mind.

"Red leather!" Frank groaned and sat up. She dropped her head into her hands. "A miniskirt," she said with a bitter laugh. "She didn't even have the legs for a maxi-dress!" And what sort of name was Miranda Parsons-Wright for a skinny, bottle-blonde, middle-aged secretary from a temping agency, anyway?

Stomping across the bedroom Frank walked into the en-suite and looked at herself in the mirror. Her short, thick, dark hair was disarrayed. An explosion in a mattress. Her skin looked sallow. There were dark circles beneath her large eyes. She stuck out her tongue. It was the same shade of yellow as when she used to smoke twenty a day.

"And don't you even think about turning cold on me today." She glared at the shower cubicle as she pulled off her vest top and shorts.

Dressed in jeans and a T shirt, her hair still damp and her feet bare, Frank stopped at the top of the stairs. She stooped and picked up Georgie's fire engine. It was the large one that made a siren sound like manic laughter. She carried it into his room and placed it carefully on top of the mound of his overflowing toybox. Setting off its jackass microchipped sound was not an option.

Frank looked around the room and sighed. The paw patrol bedding was neat and smooth. A pair of small pyjamas were folded and sat on the end of the bed. A lonely sock lay on the blue carpeted floor. Her son's absence was another reason for her to hate night shifts. Farming him out to her Mum three days a week was a necessary evil. Allowing her to work and sleep. Some hope! The silence that descended when her son was away was a hole in her life.

Frank sat at the kitchen table while the coffee machine gurgled and chuntered to itself. She flicked through the pile of mail she had retrieved from the hall. Junk, all of it. And the Salvation Army. Hadn't she given them at Christmas? There was no response to the recent job application she had submitted. The closing date had been a week ago. She dropped the pile of envelopes into the recycling box beside the kitchen bin and poured herself a mug of coffee.

"Frances, must you always slam that door!?" Frank's Mum's voice came from the living room as Frank stepped into the hall of her Mother's home.

"I don't want Daisy to get out," Frank called in reply.

As if to illustrate the point a sandy coated Cavapoo shot out of the living room and did a Scooby-Doo impression as it scrabbled for traction across the polished wooden floor of the hall. Finally, finding grip, the dog shot towards Frank like a bouffant projectile.

"And don't get that dog so excited," Sylvia Blake's voice rose in volume, "it'll ruin my laminate!"

Frank stood still and looked at the ceiling as she took a long breath. "She's doing fine without my encouragement," she told her mother.

The small dog hopped from one back paw to the other as it circled Frank batting her thighs with its front feet. Doing what amounted to a quick-step-waltz around and over the dog Frank made it to the living room without tripping.

"Mummee!" George looked up from his seat on the sofa and pushed a picture book from his lap. "Sally ated Plague Dough!" he sprang up onto his feet on the seat and bounced. A one third replica of his departed father his fair hair flopped about and his blue eyes twinkled.

"Georgie," Sylvia Blake said as she snatched at her carefully placed cushions as the bouncing dislodged them from their artistically arranged stations. "What have we said about bouncing? And you, sit!" she concluded in a sergeant major tone, causing the still manic Daisy to collapse to the floor in a cow-eyed funk.

"Plague Dough, hey?" Frank crossed the immaculate carpet and dropped onto the sofa, one arm encircling her son. "That'll teach her." She smiled and pulled the wriggling boy towards her.

"Frances, you look exhausted," Sylvia looked down at Frank and clutched one of her cushions to her breast.

Frank looked up at the thirty-years-older version of herself, the thick dark hair showing a hint of uncovered grey, the elongated, pale skinned, oval face with the faint crow's feet around the dark eyes. "Mum," she said in a tone of voice she had used since her teens, "not now, please. I'm tired enough." She kissed the top of Georgie's head as he wriggled free, intent on grabbing a small fire engine that his bouncing had uncovered behind a cushion.

"I'm only saying," Sylvia sighed and placed her precious soft furnishing on a high-backed chair. "They shouldn't be making you work all these nights when you are on your own."

"I'm a nurse, Mum. It's what we do. I have to do my share. It's only for three weeks." She watched her son trundle the small red vehicle across the sofa towards her hoping this conversation was not going where she knew it was.

"If you had only-"

"Please," Frank jumped in, "not the Sheffield Uni talk again. Not today. That was almost fifteen years ago!"

"Well!?" Sylvia held Frank's gaze then looked away and said quietly, "I mean it's not as if…"

"I was a real nurse?" Frank folded her arms as she sat back on the sofa.

Sylvia busied herself picking up Georgie's fallen book. "They should have men working in that place, not girls," she said.

"It's a mental hospital, Mum," Frank said, "not bloody Alcatraz!" She closed her eyes and sighed. It was a conversation they had kicked about too many times. "Has Georgie eaten? What's for dinner?" she asked to get away from the topic.

"Toad in the hole," Sylvia shook her head at her daughter and turned towards the door and the kitchen. "Your Father would say the same…" the words were spoken quietly in the kitchen but they still reached Frank. Like a barbed spear.

"Oh nice," Frank said without enthusiasm. She looked at Georgie and grimaced as she wiggled her fingers. "Floppy pink sausages in cardboard," she said.

The boy laughed and fell against her.

Frank squeezed her VW Polo into the last parking space outside the hospital and climbed out. Her bulging shoulder bag stuck in the tight opening between the door and frame and she tugged it free. She looked at the car taking up all the space beside her, the wheels over the dividing white line.

"Drug dealer!" she said and kicked the rear tyre of the large, black BMW.

When she pressed the button on her key fob the indicators of her car flashed, spilling yellow light onto the dark surface of the small carpark. The entrance to the hospital was fifteen metres away, warm lighting glowing inside the glass porch covering the original steps and doorway of the old building. To either side of Frank the two-storey building stretched away into the growing darkness of the evening. On the right the windows were illuminated on both floors. Some covered by thin patterned curtains. To the left the building was in darkness. The wards deserted and cold as the exodus of patients to the new hospital progressed.

Frank looked up as a bell chimed. Above the entrance the clock tower, one of the few remaining features of what had once been the Victorian County Asylum, marked the hour. It was a quarter to nine. The clock had been wrong for as long as Frank could remember. No one was going to fix it now.

Frank smiled and nodded to a few familiar faces leaving the building as she stepped inside. She shrugged her bag higher on her shoulder as she began to walk down the long entrance corridor. Office doors to each side closed and locked for the night.

"Hey, Frank, hang on."

Frank turned to see Ben Shelton fast-walking towards her from the entrance. He was tall and thin with a faint beard and long hair dragged back into a pony tail. He was one of the nursing assistants working with her.

"Hi, Ben," Frank said.

"You hear about Mick?" Ben asked falling into step beside her.

"Mick?"

"Mick Draper," Ben explained, "the Para-Porter."

"Oh, him," Frank frowned and shook her head. "What about him?"

They reached the end of the corridor, a T junction, and turned right. Another long stretch of fluorescent lit, arched ceiling tunnel ahead of them.

"Vanished last night," Ben told her. "Just walked out in the middle of the night. No one seen him since."

"They try looking inside Maureen Donner?" Frank asked.

Ben laughed and pushed her so that she staggered against the wall. "Naughty," he said and looked over his shoulder. "You'll get in trouble."

"Ben," Frank answered with a dead-pan expression, "I'm so tired I don't care. I'd welcome the sack. I'd even get in it."

"Slept like a log, me," Ben said and grinned.

"Lucky you."

"You think him and Maureen really go at it on a night?" Ben asked in a lower voice.

"You think the Pope shops in the Vatican Tesco Express?" Frank replied.

They reached the entrance to the ward and Frank tugged her key, on the extendable cord, from her belt.

"I hope that girl over the other side isn't going to be going on all night again," Ben said. "I don't fancy spending half the night over there listening to all that again."

"They must have got something into her by now," Frank said as she pulled the heavy door open.

"She had Acuphase yesterday," Ben answered. "Still awake all night."

"Maybe she's gone to HDU," Frank offered. The High Dependency Unit was the logical place for a very distressed and disturbed patient. "That girl is very ill."

"Closed to referrals till they decant to the new building," Ben said. "Orders of Mister Lawless himself."

"I thought this was a hospital," Frank said as she closed the door behind them.

3

Jack Trent opened his eyes and looked up at the ceiling. The suspended tiles above him were grey in the half light of the dormitory. The ceiling was the furthest he could see, closed in as he was by the curtains around his bed and the wardrobe and drawers standing eighteen inches from his bedside. He sat up on the bed and turned and rested his back against the wall to his right.

What had woken him?

Jack sat and listened to the sounds coming from the other seven beds around him. A couple of rattling, grunting snores. Breathing. The soft sigh of wind from outside the high windows behind the beds across the dormitory. From outside the room, down a corridor, a brief burst of laughter. Then something else. A soft creaking and an almost inaudible gasp.

Jack stood at the side of his bed and pulled down his T shirt. It had ridden up while he had been asleep. He pulled the soft cotton of his shorts free from the crack of his buttocks. Rubbing a hand over his short cropped brown hair he grimaced and stuck his tongue out. His mouth was dry, there was a taste of metal in his mouth. He coughed quietly.

"Zopiclone," he spat the word out under his breath.

Pushing aside the curtain Jack stepped from his bed area into the room. The other beds were surrounded by curtains. At the opposite end of the room to his bed two wooden doors, windows in the top quarter, separated the dorm from the corridor. Outside the lights were on and two squares of yellow glowed on the carpeted floor of the bedroom. The air in the room was cool, but not cold.

Over to Jack's right, from the last bed before the doors, behind the thin floral-patterned curtains, the soft creaking continued. Jack crossed the room and pushed the curtains apart slightly with the back of his hand, the split in the material a dark, elongated V, tapering towards the ceiling.

"Can't you do that in the frigging toilets!?" Jack said in a harsh whisper.

The activity causing the duvet to rise and fall on the bed ceased and the dark shape of a head lifted from the pillow.

"Do one, Trent!" A nasal voice hissed at Jack from the bed.

Muttering to himself Jack pushed through the doors into the corridor and turned left. Maybe it had not been the sound of one hand clapping that had woken him, he realised. The signals reaching his brain from his bladder were increasing in urgency.

Jack followed the passageway passed the doors to a few side rooms and turned another sharp left towards the toilets. Straight ahead was the small night lounge and the staff office. Before that a door led into another dormitory and a narrower corridor took a right turn to the bathrooms.

He could remember when this upper floor had just been one ward. Now it was a warren of subdivided areas, dormitories and single rooms, the sleeping area for the large ward downstairs. The Harbour they had named the ward, dispensing with the old ward names in a spirit of modernisation. What was now a maze-like expanse over two storeys had once been two separate, more comfortable patient areas. As he entered the toilet block another ripple of laughter and a raised voice reached him from the staff down in the office.

As Jack unburdened himself in one of the cubicles he heard shuffling footsteps pass behind him. Someone else awake. Jack finished his business and gave a soft smile. Two people up made the staff relenting on the no tea at night rule more of a possibility.

The toilet area was empty when Jack stepped out of the cubicle. There was no sound. Someone sitting waiting for nature to take its course he guessed. He turned to walk out.

"Excuse me," the soft voice came from behind Jack.

Turning back Jack found himself facing an elderly man. He was in daywear, a very dated suit, white shirt and thin striped tie. The man's face was very pale, long with large wet, sad eyes. A few strands of grey hair were scraped across his bald pate. Jack did not recognise him so assumed he was a new admission.

"You're up and ready a bit early, young fellow," Jack said with a smile, "it's the middle of the night."

The old man took a step forward and Jack caught the distinct aroma of pipe tobacco. It took him back to his childhood and his Grandfather.

"Do you know?" The man asked Jack.

Jack frowned. "Know what?" he asked.

Raising a white arthritic hand to his face the man stared at Jack. He fingered his trembling lower lip and looked back over both shoulders. "No one knows," he said.

"That'll include me as well then," Jack said. "Come on," he turned and beckoned the man to follow, "we'll go and cadge a cup of tea. Maybe the staff will know," he concluded with a friendly wink.

Just for an instant the old man's eyes seemed to clear and flare as they burned with a new intensity.

Jack moved off and pushed open the swing door to the corridor.

"Bloody hell, Jack!" Frank Blake stepped hastily back from the door in surprise. "I thought you were a flipping ghost. Didn't hear you come down here."

Jack smiled at her. "Nervous, aren't you?" he said.

"What're you doing up?" Frank asked.

Jack pointed over his shoulder with his thumb. "What do think I'm doing, having a barbecue?"

She laughed.

"We thought we'd come and beg a cuppa," Jack said, "me and my mate here." He turned and looked back.

There was no one there.

"Jack?" Frank asked as Jack back tracked through the toilet block pushing open cubicle doors.

Jack stopped when he reached the last empty cubicle. He looked at Frank and rubbed the back of his hand across his mouth.

"I suppose a brandy's out of the question?" he said.

4

"Hypnogogic hallucination," Frank said, "a common thing. Associated with sleep. A misinterpretation of things. An illusion."

"Sleep walking," Jack Trent said.

"Not quite, but similar I suppose," Frank nodded. "Not fully awake."

"I was awake enough to see Mark Pickering knocking one out in the dorm," Jack said in a frustrated tone.

Frank smiled as she looked at him sitting opposite her in the lounge. He was tall and slim. His very short fair hair topped a lean face with blue eyes that were framed by laughter lines, a long nose and a wide, thin lipped mouth. He held his mug of tea in two hands in his lap.

"I'll admit I sometimes let the trolley slip from under me, Frank," Jack added, "but I don't make a habit of talking to old men who aren't there."

Frank sighed and sat back in her chair. It was three o'clock in the morning. She had stumbled through the handover after coming on duty. Her eyes had drifted in their sockets as she listened to Angela Simpson, the clinical lead, tell her about the day's events. She had scanned the white board holding the names of the twenty-odd male patients on the ward and thought nothing has changed, Angela, please stop talking. Now, when she needed sleep the most, here was Jack Trent. Thirty-something, Jack. Pleasant enough with regular medication inside him. Wild and fiery when he felt his bipolar condition was his to manage without the need of his prescribed drugs. Jack. With what amounted to a ghost story.

"That man you described is not a patient on this ward," Frank said calmly. "You said something reminded you of your Granddad. Maybe that's it. You were half a sleep and thinking of him."

Ben lent forward from his chair beside Frank. "There was no one there, Jack," he reinforced.

Jack gave a grunt of exasperation and sipped his tea. "Sooner they knock this place down, the better," he said.

"A few months' time it'll be a pile of rubble," Ben said.

"Good riddance," Jack said.

When Jack had gone back to bed Frank stood and walked across the lounge. It was a small room, walls lined by old wooden armed, vinyl seat chairs. Two walls were windowed, covered now by thin patterned curtains. A dark TV sat in one corner. Pushing aside a curtain to look out all Frank could see was her own, pale, hollow eyed face staring back.

"What do you think, Ben?" she asked.

"What you said," Ben replied. "Hypnogoogle. Sleep walking."

Frank turned and leant against the window ledge. She folded her arms. Ben was sorting through a rucksack on the chair beside him. He pulled out a family size bag of crisps and a thick, dog-eared paperback book.

"What you reading," Frank asked, "The Prisoner of the Philosopher's Secret Stone Chamber?" She knew his taste in books.

"Oh, you mock," he said and laughed. "Those books are all best sellers."

"Or at least based on them," Frank shook her head. "You ever seen a ghost, Ben?" she asked.

"Yea, you on a night shift."

Frank wiggled her fingers and made a quivering woo-hoo sound. "Give us a crisp or I'll haunt you," she said.

An hour later Frank made one of her regular tours of the wards sleeping quarters. She quietly opened the doors of the side rooms, listened to heavy breathing and snores and stood at the foot of every curtained bed in the dormitories. Everyone, including Jack Trent, appeared to be in the Land of Nod.

Frank headed back toward the lounge. Then stopped at the turning for the bathrooms. The air held the definite scent of tobacco smoke. A heavy, fragrant aroma.

During her career Frank had caught people smoking odd things in odd places at odd times. That had included cannabis, heroin and once, for reasons beyond her, banana skin. Perhaps it was down to Jack, but Frank was sure what she could smell was pipe tobacco.

"Anyone down here?" Frank asked pushing open the door to the toilet block.

The short corridor and rank of half open and closed doors was silent. At the far end of the passageway a small, high window was a dark square of night. Frank stepped back and let the swing door close with a muted flap. She walked back to the lounge.

"Frank can you go over and help them out with that girl for an hour?" Maureen Donner asked. "Fiona's at her wits end and needs a break."

Frank looked at the night manager and nodded her head.

Maureen was closing in on retirement but still had a firm, lean figure. Her shoulder length brown hair was brushed back and fell in waves around her lined, tanned face. She looked apologetic as she gazed at Frank.

"I've been there half the night and a spell would be good," Maureen added.

"Yea, sure," Frank said, "we're all quiet." She unclipped the bunch of keys from her belt and handed them over.

Frank closed the connecting door between the male and female sleeping areas and locked it behind her. She was glad the journey did not require her to negotiate the lower floor, dark and empty as it would be now. In spite of the common-sense explanation she had offered, Frank realised that Jack's little old man was lingering in her memory like a...well, like a ghost, she admitted to herself.

5

The female half of the upper floor of the Harbour was almost a mirror image of the male section. Dormitories, side rooms, everything the same, but the opposite way around. Frank followed the muted sound of a TV along half-lit passageways until she reached the small lounge.

"Oh, Frank, I'm glad to see you." Fiona Moore looked up from flicking through a magazine as Frank appeared. She was a little older than Frank, early forties. Her chubby face was surrounded by a short bob of fair hair. Her eyes, behind the square frames of her glasses looked tired.

"You should have called me earlier," Frank said, "and you should have more staff if that girl's on constant."

Fiona stood and smoothed the front of her dark trousers. "She's not," she told Frank. "I just feel happier keeping an eye on her. She doesn't sleep. She catnaps during the day and part of the night. The rest of the time she sits on her bed talking constantly. It's like she's answering questions. Psychotic Mastermind. She's started and she can't finish."

Frank smiled. "Meds?" she asked simply.

Fiona rolled her eyes. "Acuphase. Regular Quetiapine. Nothing touches her."

"Who's with her now?" Frank looked over her shoulder towards the corridor to the dormitories.

"Joyce, and even her famous patience is getting ruffled."

"I'll sit with her," Frank said.

"Thanks, Frank," Fiona gave a weary smile. "Even half an hour to give our ears a rest."

"What's Maureen been doing?" Frank asked as they walked down the corridor.

Fiona pulled a sour expression. "She's done a bit," she said. "Sat in the lounge looking at rota sheets mostly, while Joyce and I spell each other. She helped with the night meds."

"Did you hear Mick the Militia disappeared during his shift last night?" Frank asked.

"Maureen may have mentioned it," Fiona said with a wink and they both laughed.

Before they reached the side rooms Fiona stopped and put her hand lightly on Frank's arm. "Sorry, Frank," she said, "I forgot. Do you know anything about Emily?"

"Only from hearsay," Frank answered. "Nineteen, psychotic."

Fiona looked quickly up and down the empty corridor as a nod to confidentiality.

"It's her second admission. Admitted yesterday," she said. "Last time it seemed like it was an extreme grief reaction to losing her Grandma. She was distressed and kept saying she could see the old lady all the time. What it looks like is that was the beginning of a psychotic illness. This time around she is responding constantly to hallucinations. She says it's people she doesn't know. Spirits."

"Shouldn't she have gone to HDU, if she needs one to one?" Frank asked.

"Not happening because they are preparing to move to the new build," Fiona replied, "and Emily is manageable, according to the Fat Useless Lump." She made ironic quotation marks with her fingers when she said manageable.

Frank shook her head and smiled. The description of John Lawless, the hospital manager, was cruelly accurate she thought.

They were about fifteen paces from the open door of the side-room when Frank heard Emily's voice.

"I don't know. I keep telling you." The voice was light but there was an edge beneath the surface. The sound of someone reaching the end of tolerance, about to snap. "I don't know what that is. That was a long time ago, I think. No, they won't do that. Things are different now. Please, one at a time!"

Frank looked at Fiona.

"It just goes on," the older woman said and shrugged her shoulders.

Joyce was a fifty-plus woman with a slightly mannish, handsome face. She sported a hairstyle she had maintained since the eighties. As Frank and Fiona approached she stood up from her chair before the open door and sighed. "You must be the cavalry, Frances," she said. Her eyes looked tired and her face more lined than Frank remembered.

"Go flop and drink tea," Frank said smiling. Joyce was one of the few people who used her proper name.

Fiona turned and headed back towards the lounge as Joyce put her hand on Frank's shoulder. "How's your Mum?" she asked. "I haven't seen her in a while."

Frank's mother's need for occasional spiritual comfort had brought the two women into contact through the Spiritualist Church. Frank's own cynicism about that was currently on hold.

"Oh, she's coping," Frank answered with a small laugh. "She looks after George for me a lot. I think he keeps her focused on more earthly matters."

Joyce laughed quietly. "Children are good at that," she said.

"Tell me about it," Frank acknowledged. "He doesn't give either of us much time to feel sorry for ourselves."

Joyce smiled and turned away. Frank turned and looked at Emily.

The narrow side room, bed, wardrobe, drawers and high, curtained window was illuminated only by the light from the corridor. On the metal framed bed the girl sat with her knees encircled by her arms. She was very thin with long dark hair framing a pale face with large dark eyes and an upturned nose above the perfect cupid's bow of her pink lips. She was wearing pink pyjamas with a white pattern depicting clouds and leaping lambs.

"Emily," Frank said as she sat in the chair in the doorway.

Emily stopped talking and looked at Frank.

"You not sleepy?" Frank asked.

The girl looked at Frank with an unblinking stare. "They won't let me sleep," she said. "The dark frightens them."

"Who are we talking about?"

"You shouldn't have come here," Emily said. Her eyes looked over Frank's shoulder and her expression hardened momentarily.

"Why's that?" Frank asked.

"Because…" Her voice faded and she turned her face to the wall.

After that the girl refused to respond to Frank. She lowered her eyes and continued to talk to herself in a quieter tone. Once she looked up and gazed passed Frank to the empty door way then dropped her eyes again.

Frank pressed her thumbs against her eyes and rested back in the chair. It's going to be a long hour she thought and yawned.

6

After the handover Frank paused outside the entrance to the hospital and took a huge breath of the cold morning air. Her level of tiredness was off the scale and her mouth felt as though it were stuffed with cotton wool. Shrugging her bag higher on her shoulder she walked to her car as she pressed the key fob. Standing at the side of the car she looked back at the glass enclosed doors of the building.

In the five years since she had qualified Frank had only left work a handful of times worried about any of the patients in her care. She was fortunate in being able to switch off and not take the woes of her charges away with her usually. As she started her car Frank added the girl in the pink pyjamas to her list of worries. Whatever the Harbour was doing to help Emily Greene, it was not working.

Frank drove her car on automatic pilot, negotiating the increasing morning traffic under a grey, cloud-heavy October sky. She registered the faces of passing drivers fleetingly. People looking relaxed before whatever their day had in store for them happened. She wondered how many of them, like her, sometimes worried if what they had signed up for was actually what they ended up doing. Did other people feel that the organisation employing them had lost its way?

In her five years as a staff nurse it was only in the last year that Frank had begun to feel that something was out of step. She had never aspired to be God's gift to nursing. All she had ever wanted was to do her job and help people. Naïve, she realised now. She was a small cog in a mechanism that would grind on with or without her presence.

A wave of tiredness made her shiver as she halted at traffic lights. She turned on the heater. In a car beside her a woman was talking on a phone while looking in the rear-view mirror and applying lipstick.

It was the Harbour that had tipped the scales, Frank thought.

Under the guidance of John Lawless the hospital had abandoned a multi-ward approach for a lumbering amalgamation of the male and female wards. The new design was supposed to be more practical, make better use of resources and allow for more therapeutic activities. What John had ignored was the fact that it was a model that had failed everywhere else it had been tried. Adapting existing wards into one created an unmanageable labyrinth. An expanse where observation and patient safety overrode any other duties the staff tried to pursue. The Harbour became the work and the patients the hinderance. After a few months the exodus of experienced staff had started. People who cared chased after community posts or moved away to areas where they could care for their patients, not spend their days counting and penning them. Frank had found herself surrounded by few people more experienced than herself and many, ambitious and newly qualified, eager to advance and reluctant to challenge John Lawless' empire building.

The only good thing was that, like the hospital, the Harbours days were now numbered.

Frank yawned and recognised her rambling thoughts as another sign of her tiredness. She focused on the road as the last mile of her journey home began. Forget work she told herself. Last night shift done. Three days off. She turned the heater down. The car had warmed up and something was starting to smell a little.

Frank sniffed. She hoped something wasn't going to burn out. A repair bill she could do without. But there was a definite smell. Almost like tobacco burning.

When she pulled onto the drive after getting home Frank sat for a moment in the quiet of the car and gazed at her house. The burning smell had faded as the heat dissipated from the vehicle. No repair bill. She felt relaxed and ready for sleep. She would settle for whatever she got and look forward to the whole night in bed. She looked up at her bedroom window and thought of the bed waiting beyond it.

The tiled floor beneath her bare feet was cold. Frank looked up from the floor and someone behind her grabbed a handful of her hair.

"Watch those teeth, she's a biter!" a male voice said. The sound echoed loudly.

Frank tried to see who was speaking but struggled to move. Each side of her a person was holding her arms outstretched. A man and a woman, both covered from chest to shin by stained leather or rubber aprons. The fingers in her hair remained locked in place. She kicked her legs and the rough cotton gown she was wearing lifted. Cold air swam around her legs. Frank looked around as she attempted to pull her arms free.

They were in a large tiled bathroom. Exposed pipework decorated the walls. There were heavy glass globes on sconces on the walls from which sickly yellow light glowed. Ahead were three large metal bath tubs standing on clawed feet bolted to the floor. The taps were ridiculously antiquated and cumbersome looking. A length of thick, flat hose snaked across the floor. Its surface had darkened in one section where it lay in a pool of water.

The grip on her hair released and a man walked around in front of her. He had a long face, swept back grey hair and a bristling moustache. His eyes were almost hidden in the creases of an unpleasant smile. Like the others he was encased in a long dirty apron.

"Right, Madam," he said and made a come forward gesture to his companions. "Bath time!"

Frank was about to utter a string of obscenities when she registered the other sound echoing throughout the room. A high-pitched shrieking that she could not believe she had not noticed before. Because it was her. Screaming.

Twisting her torso and trying to bend her legs Frank fought as the three raised her into the air in a position suitable for crucifixion. Then she fell suddenly. The positions of the restraining hands on her body changed as she was plunged into a bath of ice cold water and held below the surface.

"Good God!" Frank gasped as her eyes sprang open. She lay on the bed and stared up at the grinning clown. Her heart was thumping like a boxing gym speed ball.

Without bothering to glance at the digital clock Frank got out up and walked out of the bedroom. If that was the quality of sleep she was going to have after a night of psychotic rambling and ghost stories she would rather sit and drink tea and stare blankly at daytime TV.

At the top of the stairs, her dream, day mare, still circulating in her head, Frank stooped automatically and picked up Georgie's fire engine. After replacing it on the overflowing mound of his toybox she went downstairs and filled the kettle.

7

Jack chewed a piece of cold toast as he gazed around the dining area on the ground floor of the Harbour. Men sat engrossed in cooked breakfasts, cups of tea and coffee. The room was filled with the sound of subdued chatter and the clatter and clink of cutlery and pottery. Outside the tall windows a few leafless trees moved in the wind beneath a heavy, grey sky. In the distance, beyond the carpark and what had once been a football pitch, traffic moved back and forth on the main road. Jack pushed his plate away, ignoring the other half of his slice of toast, and sipped tea from his cup.

He had not slept much after getting up for the toilet. He had stayed on his bed, dozing occasionally as he mulled over what he had seen. He had feigned sleep the twice he had heard Frank Blake enter the dormitory as she did her Nightingale routine. He had nothing else to say to her. He had not been sleepwalking. The alternative annoyed him. It went against everything he believed about how the world worked.

Waiting for the morning medication round Jack sat in the dayroom. Mark Pickering, tall, overweight, his two chins covered by the dark stubble of a half-grown beard, glared at him as he passed carrying a dripping cup of coffee.

"What you staring at, Trent?" Mark asked in his nasal whine.

"Just noticed you've got Popeye's right arm and Olive Oyl's left," Jack answered with a twisted smile on his thin lips.

Mark took a step closer and stared down at Jack in his seat. "You're a peeping tom," he said. "Pervert!"

"Oh, it gives me great pleasure watching you bang one out, Mark," Jack told him, glad of a reason to vent frustration. "Who were you thinking about, Sooty or Sweep?"

The hand holding the coffee moved slightly. The cup tilting towards Jack.

"Do it, Mark," Jack said coldly, his smile gone, "and your lover will be encased in plaster from knuckles to shoulder by tonight."

The man spat a short expletive and turned away.

Jack sighed and looked around the motley collection of men standing and sitting around the room. They ranged in age from a late teen to pushing pensions. They were casually dressed in a mix of styles from tracksuits to too old and fat for jeans. Some were chatting, a couple laughing, some sat staring at their pasts or uncertain futures. The only thing we have in common is faulty wiring, Jack thought.

"Three bloody weeks," Jack said to himself and rubbed his nose between his tired eyes.

Things had started going wrong for Jack before Claire died, but it had been slapping the vicar, knocking him backwards into Claire's grave, that had ended with him back in hospital detained under Section Three of the Mental Health Act. For the third time in his life.

Jack and Claire had been divorced for a year when the cancer she had beaten into submission three years earlier returned. Neither of them had moved on much. Jack was still subject to the fluctuations in his mental health that had eventually rung the bell on Claire's tolerance and their marriage. Claire had devoted herself to being a working Mum and the care of their daughter, Charlotte. Jack moved back into the family home to provide support and they agreed to be practical, avoid useless emotions and fight together.

The reality was, Jack watched the woman he still loved change from a lively, curvy brunette into a child's drawing stickman. Claire faded away and became a shadow of herself. Then disappeared when the sun went behind a cloud.

At some point during the nine months journey from diagnosis to Claire's death Jack had stopped taking his medication. He felt better able to cope, had more energy, without the dulling of his mind he felt the drugs caused. With hindsight Jack admitted that he was a selfish bastard, and needed the edge his elevating mood gave him to prepare to face the pain and loss bearing down on him like a speeding locomotive.

The pious banality he had heard in the vicar's voice at the funeral was the catalyst needed for Jack to let go of the reins that had been steadily slipping from his hands.

After three weeks in hospital, back on a combination of mood stabilising drugs, Jack was not completely whole again, but was getting there. He recognised the sharp edge to his tongue and the quickness of his mind to provide him barbed comments for what they were. Part of the shield protecting him from his true emotions. He could live with that for now.

"Don't take too long, Jack," the voice sounded hollowly in the stairwell. "We're supposed to keep this door locked as much as possible."

Jack paused on the half-landing of the dogleg stairs on his way up to the dormitories. "I'm getting a jumper, not knitting one. How long do you think I'm going to be?" he told the nursing assistant.

At the top of the stairs Jack paused. Down the corridor leading to the female dorms one of the cleaning staff, in a yellow tunic, was pulling a vacuum cleaner as she moved over the floor. A long black cable trailed behind her and disappeared through a narrow opening in the door to the female ward. She raised a hand to Jack and he offered a half salute in response.

Apart from the whining drone of the vacuum it was quite in the sleeping areas. It was away from the constant traffic and voices of the ground floor. Jack could easily have gone back to bed.

He stopped at the entrance to the toilet block and stared at the rough white surface of the closed door. He thought about what had happened during the night. There was nothing he could do about it he decided. Bugger it! Chalk it up to the further joys of being locked up.

Jack was pulling a jumper from his cupboard in the dormitory when he heard raised voices. It sounded like a couple of different people. He could not make out what they were saying until a female voice called clearly.

"Emily!"

Jack walked back into the corridor and leant around the corner. A woman was walking towards him. She was stocky with a round face and short bobbed hair. She wore the classic dark trousers and dull coloured top of the staff's non-uniform uniform.

"Is there a girl down here?" the woman asked.

Behind her, down the corridor, another woman, slimmer, short fair hair, was standing, hands on hips.

Jack stepped into the passageway. "Only Charlize Theron, and we're busy," he said.

"What? Oh," the woman said, "don't be stupid. A young girl, dark hair?"

Jack shook his head.

"Here!" the woman furthest away said and pointed into the toilet area.

The stocky woman backtracked and they both disappeared into the short corridor to the washrooms.

Jack reached the turning, his arms in the sleeves of his jumper and the body stretched across his chest, when the two women emerged from the toilets. The swing door batted back and forth behind them. Between the pair a young girl wriggled and kicked her legs.

The girl was small and very thin. She was wearing jeans and a pink T shirt. Her long dark hair whipped across her pale face as she fought with the two nurses.

"They need to stop," the girl said. "I can't keep doing it."

"We need to go back to the ward, Emily," the fair-haired woman told the girl. Her voice was firm but not unkind. She and the stocky woman had the girl's arms in tight grips.

As the threesome turned towards the exit the girl craned her neck and looked back at Jack. "They just want to know," she said and her large dark eyes fastened on Jack's. "Do you know?" she asked him.

"No one knows," Jack said quietly to himself.

8

Frank dropped Georgie's Paw Patrol backpack on the floor of the hall and closed the front door. She flipped on the lights in the hall and landing and ushered George towards the stairs. After an afternoon with her mother Frank was ready for some alone time. Bath Georgie, story, bed, then flop in front of the TV.

The running water reminded Frank of her dream. She frowned as she tested the temperature of her son's bath. The ancient, cruel spa treatment had obviously been dragged from her mind from something she had read about old psychiatric practices. No doubt partly thanks to Jack Trent and his ghosts. It had been frightening, but Frank's frown was more about her own responses in the dream. All that screaming. Frank did not do helpless.

After his bath, and a discussion about where the chickens in Grandma's stew came from, Frank settled on Georgie's bed beside him and read from one of his books.

It was The Enormous Turnip, which at four and a half he was maybe getting a little old for. George liked it because he could delay the process by offering ever more elaborate ways of getting the mutant vegetable from the ground, and so prolong the story. After finally agreeing that tying a rope around the turnip attached to a spaceship would work, Frank kissed her son, patted his duvet and went downstairs.

Frank prowled across the tiled floor of her large square kitchen. She trailed her hand across the oak cupboard fronts then stood tapping her fingers against the fridge door. She was not hungry, but had a craving she thought she should resist. She had already drunk one bottle of wine since the weekend. It was a habit she needed to watch, she thought. She was not a great fan of drinking alone, but it had crept up since Pete left.

The sudden bizarre thought of her ex-husband in the arms of Parsons-Wright from rent a floozy swayed Frank. She carried her glass of red wine into the lounge, placed it on a low table and dropped onto the large sofa. Pulling her bare feet up onto the seat she toggled the TV remote.

The end credits of EastEnders rolled before a spritely pair of presenters began pursuing the sellers of dodgy dog food on some consumer programme. Frank's eyes were rolling before she found out whether the poisoned Shih-Tzu lived or died.

Frank came awake slowly to find she was pinned to the sofas arm cushion by a weight on her left side. The TV was displaying a news report. The weight pressing on her legs and left arm was Georgie, fast asleep, a fire engine upside down in his lap.

Frank extricated her arm while she muted the TV. She brushed her son's fringe away from his eyes and moved around so that his head was cradled by her arm. His eyes opened slowly.

"Hello, you," Frank said, smiling. "What are you doing here?"

Georgie blinked his huge blue eyes. He yawned. "I didn't like the man," he said.

Frank stroked his face. "What man, Buster?"

Georgie did not answer. He raised his hand and pointed at the open door to the hall. It was dark beyond the doorway. Just visible through the stair rails was the soft glow of a plug-in night light on the landing.

"The Granddad," Georgie answered. "He keeped opening all the doors."

Frank felt the prickle of goose flesh creep across her arms. She looked into the dark hall. She lifted her son and he knelt beside her on the sofa. "Just a dream, mate," she said, "let's get back to bed." Frank used her best take-your-medication voice. It sounded firm and confident.

Georgie shook his head and remained on the sofa. "See if he's gone."

"Right," Frank said. "I'll put the lights on then it's back to bed. It was just a dream, Georgie." Her voice had a slight edge to it and she realised it was aimed at herself for allowing the twinge of apprehension to grip her a moment ago.

Frank turned on the hall and landing lights and stood at the bottom of the stairs. The Louisville Slugger popped into her head. The baseball bat Peter had kept under his side of the bed after a spate of car break-ins around the estate. Dismissing the image, she marched up the stairs.

The doors of all three bedrooms, the toilet and the bathroom were open or ajar. The rooms in darkness, but for the glow from the landing light. Frank could not remember if they had been closed earlier or not. She looked into each room, flicking the lights on and off and closed all the doors firmly.

Frank stood at the top of the stairs and looked down at Georgie in the hall. "Okay," she said and smiled, "nobody here but us chickens."

Georgie gave a wide smile just as Frank's faded. She looked over her shoulders. The square landing was empty, brightly lit. All the doors were closed. Frank felt the cold tingle of the hairs rising on her arms again.

Faintly, but clearly, she could smell the heavy aroma of burning tobacco. The scent faded as quickly as it had arisen.

Walking down the stairs Frank convinced herself that the aroma she had registered three times now was just another effect of sleep deprivation and suggestibility. She had a serious word with herself as she turned off lights and the TV and headed Georgie up the stairs before her with a string of reassuring inanities. Too tired to argue with his large puppy-dog eyes Frank let him climb into her bed with the warning, "Just this once." Again! As Georgie snuggled under the duvet Frank turned to close the bedroom door.

Across the dark landing the door to her son's room was ajar. The door she had definitely closed a few minutes before. Frank stood with one hand on her door as she looked at what seemed too much like the silhouette of a person standing just inside the door to Georgie's room.

Frank kept her eyes on the dark shape. A head and shoulders, darker than the pale wall behind them. There was no sensation of gooseflesh this time. Just the hammering of her heart. She stepped back from the door, knelt, and with trembling fingers scrabbled for the baseball bat beneath the bed. When her fingers closed around the bat she pulled it to her and walked out onto the landing. The shadow remained in place as if transfixed by her unblinking stare.

"Who's there?" Frank said as firmly as she could manage, flicking on the landing light. The illumination revealed only a dark space between the door and frame of Georgie's room. Then very slowly the door closed. The spring latch gave a soft click as it engaged.

For a couple of seconds Frank felt that the landing was expanding, the closed door receding. Her heart skipped a beat. She gave a swift glance back at her own room and tightened her grip on the bat. The taped handle gave a creak under the pressure of her fingers as she thought of her son.

Frank advanced and turned the door handle with unsteady fingers. She kicked open the door and walked inside, bat first. The empty room sneered at her.

"Mummy!" Georgie called to her.

Frank backed out of the room and closed the door. She looked around her. All the doors were closed. The bottom of the staircase disappeared into shadow. But wasn't there something down there?

Points of light. The reflection from staring eyes. A figure in the gloom of the hall, vaguely man shaped. The pale oval of a face in shadow looking up at her. Frank blinked and the illusion vanished. Below her was her own pale coat, draped over the coat rack, light reflected from the dark buttons.

Frank walked back into her bedroom, closed the door and leant against it.

"Okay, Buster," she said, "time for sleep." There was a slight tremor in her voice and her heart was still thumping.

Half an hour later Frank lay in bed with the duvet pulled up to her chin. Georgie was nestled against her back, snoring softly. A low wattage lamp illuminated the room. Her eyes were wide open, fastened on the Louisville Slugger leaning against the bedside cabinet.

## 9

Jack sat on the side of his bed in the dormitory with the curtains of his bed area closed around him. He looked at the zopiclone tablet in the palm of his hand. He had pushed it up between his gum and top lip after putting it in his mouth, then spat it out in the dorm. Going to the toilet straight after the meds round was too much of a give-away to the staff. Jack had been around the garden too many times to be that obvious.

Jack had no objections to sleeping tablets usually. Sometimes they even helped. When you shared sleeping quarters with the likes of Mark Pickering anything helped. However, tonight Jack wanted a little time to think. During the day, on the Harbour, that was nigh on impossible. The ward was a constant stream of patients, nurses and medical staff battering backwards and forwards.

On the old, smaller wards the consultant had appeared once a week, and if you saw a doctor between times you were either raving or dying. With men from all compass points of the county locked up together on the Harbour, and four consultants overseeing their treatment, every day seemed to revolve around a ward round or review, with men arguing, haranguing the staff for leave or discharge and harried medical staff constantly searching for a nurse who knew anything about any patient.

Jack needed time to process what was brewing in his mind.

Why had the girl asked him the same question, in almost the same place, as the old man he had seen? Coincidence? That would be the logical answer. And the girl. Emily? She was clearly ill. Yet, Jack had seen the man as clear as day. Heard him and spoken to him. Then he had vanished. Jack was not someone who hallucinated. Well... there was that time after the mushrooms, but that had been a frog in a bowler hat.

Jack smiled to himself.

No, the man in the toilets had been as real as the urine puddles on the floor. If he was a ghost what did that say about Jack's view of the world? Jack had never believed that anything, anybody, continued to exist after death. If he was wrong, what did that mean? The real question for Jack was; what did that mean for Claire?

Jack pushed open the swing door into the toilet block and stepped inside. Someone, to his left in one of the cubicles, was whistling an off-tune version of Bridge Over Troubled Water while a stream of urine descended into a toilet bowl.

The toilets were on the left. On the right a few doors covered shower stalls. Straight ahead, making the block a T shape, was a door leading into a row of sinks. The actual baths of the bathroom area where back behind Jack, out of the door and to the right, in a spur corridor. The walls of the whole area were painted a uniform off-white and the doors glossed in slightly yellowing white.

"Alright, Jack?" A rotund little man dressed in checked pyjama bottoms and a grey T shirt emerged from a toilet and greeted Jack.

Jack nodded. "Terry," he said, acknowledging the man.

"Stand closer," Terry said and laughed as he pushed the swing door to exit, "it's shorter than you think."

"Like your arms," Jack said to the closing door. "Can't you reach the taps to wash your hands?"

Jack stood half way down the short passageway and looked around. It was a cold, echoing space. A narrow T with vinyl flooring and a badly plastered ceiling. Hardly a gothic mansion suitable to the appearance of spectres from the beyond.

"Why pop up down here, old man?" Jack asked. And why had the same spot attracted the girl?

Jack pushed open the door into the cross bar of the T, where the row of sinks were. He immediately registered a drop in temperature. Above the five sinks, with mirrors behind them, at the top of the wall, was a small square window. Jack walked the row of sinks as he thought about why this particular place might be significant.

Maybe ghosts just pop up in random places, he thought.

"Bollocks!" Jack suddenly felt ridiculous. What the hell was he doing, hanging around in the toilets? It was work better done in a dirty old Mac. Ghosts! Maybe three weeks in hospital was not enough.

Jack let the swing door rattle away behind him and walked back into the corridor. He felt wired. There was a buzzing sensation in the back of his head that he recognised. It did not bode well. It was the small warning tickle he often ignored before things began to spiral beyond his control. If he went to lay down now, he knew, his mind would be turning over all the garbage accumulated. Claire, ghosts, Pickering, the persistent cacophony of the ward, voices, TV. He tried to remember where he had stashed that Zopiclone tablet.

Pushing apart the curtains of one of the high windows in the corridor Jack rested his elbows on the sill and looked out at the night.

Above the dark silhouette of the hospital roof the sky was heavily populated by clouds. The twinkling pinpricks of stars were just visible between banks of cloud that were illuminated from below by the nauseous yellow glow of street lights. Jack shifted his focus and looked at his reflection in the dark glass.

"If you're thinking about jumping I'll give you a leg up," Mark Pickering said as his face appeared in the window behind Jack.

Jack looked at the face reflected in the glass. "If I have to spend many more nights with you I'll be glad of the push," he said.

Mark grunted and moved away. Jack turned his head and watched him walk down the passageway towards the toilets. A small man in striped pyjamas emerged from the dormitory door, side stepped Mark with an anxious expression and came towards

Jack. He had a towel over one shoulder and was clutching a toothbrush and toothpaste in one hand.

"Hello, Jack," the man said. He was middle aged, short, with a round, florid face and greying hair. He wore checked, purple slippers.

Jack nodded. "Hiya, Bernard," he said.

Bernard looked back over his shoulder. "He's a bad temper so-and-so," he said.

"Mark?" Jack smiled at the little man. "Born with his knickers in a twist."

Bernard leant towards Jack. "He used to go to the toilet in a carrier bag in his wardrobe," he said in a hushed voice.

"Nothing would surprise me, Bernard," Jack answered.

"Well, I'm just off to brush my teeth," Bernard held up his brush and tube of paste. "Night, Jack." He walked away.

Jack watched the small man approach the T junction and turn left. He was going in the opposite direction to the toilets and washrooms. A right turn would have taken him towards the door to Jack's dorm. Left was a similar dead end, passed a few side room doors. Frowning, Jack stepped up to the junction.

Jack looked to his right. A few side room doors to one side, the door to Jack's dorm on the other. Straight ahead the corridor ended in a dead end made by the doors of a large linen cupboard. Jack turned and looked the other way. No sign of Bernard. Side room doors one side, a few curtained windows opposite.

Jack could hear water running faintly and remembered that the last door across the junction, beyond the side rooms, was a toilet with a small sink. Jack never used it. It was out of the way and he assumed mainly for the use of the men in the rooms down that spur of the ward.

The door of the toilet swung open and Bernard appeared, wiping his lower face with his towel. He looked at Jack as he walked closer. He looked a little embarrassed.

"Alright, Bernard?" Jack asked.

"Yes, Jack," Bernard looked over his shoulder and gave a weak smile. "Just brushing my teeth." He rubbed his towel between his hands and his eyes avoided Jack's.

"That little loo's a bit out of your way, isn't it?" Jack asked.

Bernard looked down and fiddled with the cap of his tube of tooth paste. "Bit of privacy. You know?" he said.

It was mainly Bernard's behaviour that brought to Jack the aroma of rat. "The wash rooms are closer to your dorm," he said.

Bernard looked up at him then dropped his eyes again. "I don't like the toilet block on a night," he said.

"Really?" Jack said, thinking, "coincidence my arse."

10

After dropping Georgie off at school Frank sat in her car outside Tesco and drummed her fingers on the steering wheel. She needed to get herself organised and apply for the next community job that came up. Her recent application to the Crisis Team had obviously fallen on stony ground. Shifts, particularly night shifts, were doing her head in. Sleep deprivation was causing her weird dreams, stupid anxieties provoked by her son's nightmares and, it seemed, olfactory hallucinations, and 'hypnogoogle' illusions. After all, she had not seen anything describable, and gentle questioning had only received a repeat of Georgie's initial report. A Granddad opening doors. No details or description of the man left in his memory after sleeping.

A regular nine to five job would allow Frank to sleep every night and enable her and Georgie to get into some sort of regular routine. Even if that meant him spending a little more time each day after school with her Mum. Toad in the Hole was a price worth paying for sanity and a night's sleep, she thought.

Frank pushed her trolley into the supermarket and made a sharp turn into the book aisle. She cast her eyes over the latest bestseller shelves and frowned. She had read the recent Stephen King and been disappointed, and who really cared about Russel Brand's philosophy. Both millionaires, their views about what was scary or relevant was lightyears away from Frank's life. She picked up and read the blurb on the newest Lee Child. It sounded too familiarly like the last one. She moved on, in more of a Marian Keyes mood.

In the vegetable aisle Frank looked at the wilted bags of salad and tried to decide what greenery might persuade Georgie to indulge in food beyond the scope of chicken dippers and curly fries. What was it about the colour green kids revolted against? Had she tried him with mango?

Frank suddenly had to side step to avoid the advance of a very obese woman speeding down the thoroughfare on a bright red mobility scooter.

"Hey, don't mind me," Frank said, "I'm just walking here."

The woman swept passed without a glance at Frank.

"Maybe you should try the mangos and lay off the chips."

Apparently, the woman had heard. As she swept around the corner she raised her right hand, index and second fingers making a V sign.

"Charming," Frank said and yawned. A wave of tiredness swept over her and she stopped her trolley, put her elbow on the handle and her chin on her palm. She swept her eyes down the aisle of produce.

Suddenly she smelt the rich aroma of burning tobacco and the rows of fruit and vegetables seemed to stretch into the distance, as though she were looking down the wrong end of a telescope. The bright lighting and the sounds of voices seemed to become magnified and swelled around her. Gripping the handle of the trolley Frank shook her head and tried to take a steadying breath. Her throat and chest suddenly felt tight. She gasped air in and out, but they were shallow, unsatisfying breaths, tainted by the sickly aroma of smoke. The muscles of her chest contracted as if under the grip of an immense hand. Her throat was closing. She tried to swallow and the band of steel around her neck prevented her.

Heart attack! The thought swamped Frank's mind and she felt her knees buckle. Georgie! She thought with a mounting sense of fear and helplessness.

The other shoppers began to notice Frank's distress. Faces turned in her direction as people slowed and gawped at her. An older woman with blue-grey hair took a step backwards and caused an avalanche of bananas.

Frank stumbled forward a few steps as the trolley moved under her weight. She leant over the handle and managed to drag in air. There was no pain in her chest, a rational corner of her mind registered. She just had an overwhelming sensation of panic.

A panic attack! The realisation hit Frank with a sense of relief and, oddly, shame. She should have realised. Of all people, she should have recognised what was happening to her.

One hand on the trolley Frank managed to summon a weak smile for the onlookers as she concentrated on settling her breathing. The choking sensation and feeling of tightness abated slowly. The burning, incense aroma faded.

"It's OK," Frank said to the handful of people around her. "I'm okay. Lack of sleep," she explained unconvincingly. People began to move away.

"Are you alright?" The woman with the blue-grey, wavy hair stepped a little closer to Frank.

"Yes. Yes. Really." Frank managed a stronger smile for the concerned woman.

"I think your Granddad has gone for help," the woman said. The large blue eyes in the thin, lined face still held a trace of worry.

"Grandad?" Frank queried.

"The man who was standing with you," the woman explained, "the older man. He turned and walked away when you became ill. He's gone for help."

Frank pulled at the collar of her T shirt beneath her denim jacket. The muscles in her throat twitched as if about to tighten again. "I'm on my own," she said. Pushing the trolley away from her she turned towards the nearest exit.

In her car Frank scrolled through the list of contacts in her mobile with trembling fingers. Just adrenaline she told herself. Her thumb hovered over her Mum's number for a second. What would she say to her? What would not draw the response that it was her job to blame? Frank scrolled on. She needed one of her friends who would listen to what was on her mind.

"No!" Frank spoke to herself as her heart settled in her chest and the trembling of her hands diminished. She needed to deal with this herself.

Whatever it was.

11

Jack stood outside the front of the hospital and looked up at the clock tower. It was early afternoon but dull, the sky piled with dark clouds. The pointed spire of the tower, flecked with pigeon droppings, silhouetted against the overcast sky, looked suitably gothic. It matched Jack's thoughts. The clock displayed the wrong time, out of sync with the world. Quite appropriate, Jack decided, for its position above a mental hospital.

Jack let his eyes wander over the building. He could see clearly where the structure had been added to over the years. The older, dark brickwork contrasting with the lighter new additions. The newer parts were mainly ground floor extensions to wards. Flat roofed annexes, stuck on with no real attempt to match the masonry or windows of the original structure. The bulk of the hospital had tall windows looking into large, high ceilinged rooms. The additions were squat and workman-like with square windows and none of the style of the original Victorian design.

Jack turned and continued his stroll around the exterior of the hospital. He paid little attention to the people he passed. Staff and patients bound on various errands, or like him just making use of leave from the ward. He was still turning over last night's conversation with Bernard. He ambled along. Not aimlessly though. Bernard had given him food for thought.

Reluctantly at first, but with increasing relish, Bernard had relayed to Jack his reasons for avoiding certain areas of the ward, and the hospital as a whole. After half a lifetime of admissions Bernard had experienced odd feelings around various parts of the hospital. He had also picked up, through gossip and eavesdropping on the staff, enough anecdotes to qualify the hospital for a slot on Britain's Most Haunted.

The tales most often featured unexplained sounds and voices, self-opening doors, changes in temperature and sensations of being followed or watched. However, Bernard had also heard people discuss seeing shadowy figures and feeling the touch of hands or breath on goose-pimpled skin. Bernard's particular favourite was the story overheard one night while listening to the staff. This recounted the experience of one of the porters whose clip-on tie was snatched from his neck and hurled ahead of him down a corridor.

The setting for that story was the goal of Jack's wandering. The main rear corridor of the hospital. It was, Bernard had advised him, the place most people had reservations about entering during the night. It featured in a lot of the reports of strange sounds and sensations. It had once been the main route to the, no longer used, hospital mortuary, Bernard had concluded with a sage nod of his head.

Passing around the side of the building Jack could see, over to his left, five hundred metres away, the new hospital. The completed structure, with visible metal supports and wooden cladding, looked more like a shopping centre than what it was. Jack gave it a glance and moved on. He ignored the question in his head regarding how often he was likely to be admitted there in the future. All he wanted at the moment was to be free again. And proving to himself that hallucinating little old men was not a new phase of wackiness was important to him.

At the back of the older building Jack came upon a gated compound for staff vehicles. It was surrounded by a sturdy metal mesh fence. Just outside this there was a row of porta-loos and two heavy, bright yellow trucks, one of them equipped with a massive toothed scoop on a crane arm. The vehicles belonging to the company tasked with preparing the demolition of the hospital. Work that had already started, Jack knew, with the destruction of a freestanding structure that had once been a centre for young people.

Spotting the rear entrance Jack walked across the compound and pushed open a door to find himself in the infamous back corridor.

It was a hundred metres of blank, cold passageway. The walls were a bland magnolia, the ceiling slightly curved and the floor an expanse of heavy duty light grey vinyl. To Jack's left the exterior wall held a few windows spaced along its length. The right-hand side had old wooden doors and a few windows. Most of which, Jack noticed as he walked along, were covered by blinds inside or in one or two cases appearing to have the glass painted over.

Jack imagined the corridor at night. A cold, echoing space that had existed for the last one hundred years. The route to the morgue. It was easy to understand how its reputation had emerged.

Jack was alone in the corridor. There was the occasional echo of voices and the reverberation of closing doors now and then, but no one appeared. The sounds apparently transmitted from the adjoining corridors to the rest of the hospital. Because he was unobserved and always enquiring, Jack tried the handles of the doors he passed. All were firmly locked. Until he reached the last door.

After turning the handle and giving it a push the scarred wooden surface of the door swung open. Jack looked at the scuffed paint on a wall a metre inside the door. The dark entrance to the room was immediately to the right of the door. Leaning forward he looked into the room. He noticed a light switch on the wall, but flicking it produced no effect.

The blind covered window allowed in enough light for Jack to see some of the space inside. The room appeared to be for storage, and was a mess. The floor was littered with scattered spools of ancient tape; audio and antique video. The reels were laying across the floor in front of ranks of chest high cardboard boxes. A couple of the containers were overturned, papers and cardboard files had spilled out. Behind the cartons there was an old, glass fronted cabinet holding shelves of leather bound books. The air inside the room felt damp and cold.

Jack stepped inside and his foot contacted with something that rolled across the floor with a metallic rattle. He looked down. It was a long, black torch. A Maglite. Jack picked the light up and pressed the switch on the side of the heavy cylinder. It was dead. With the torch in his hand he stepped further into the room.

The space was L shaped. Away to Jack's left the room turned out of sight. The far corner dark where the diffused light from the covered window failed to penetrate the gloom. Jack pulled open the top of one of the boxes beside him. Inside was a stack of files, each in a damp mottled buff folder. Laying the torch down on a box top he picked up a file and opened it. He turned and carried the file over towards the window to read the inside.

Over the page from a description of the patient's age, address, gender, weight and height there were lines of neat script. Each entry was preceded by a date and time before recording observations of the patient. The writing was in faded ink. Not ballpoint, but the unmistakeable markings of a fountain pen. Flicking pages back and forth Jack got the gist. Mainly due to one page that was devoted to a record of the administration of medication.

Jack gave a soft grunt. What he was reading was the record and observations of someone who had been induced into a coma through the administration of Insulin.

Jack swung around when something behind him moved creating a rough rustling sound. He dropped the file back onto the top of the pile in the box. The sound had come from the dark corner of the room, around the bend of the L.

"Someone there?" Jack asked.

Silence was the only reply.

Jack stepped to his right as he gazed into the darker corner of the room. As his eyes adjusted to the gloom all that became partly visible were more boxes.

"Rats," Jack said quietly.

Stepping back Jack looked around the dimly lit room again. Ancient files, tapes of who knew what, and a feeling of neglect and forgotten people was all he imagined he felt. No ghosts. Nothing to prove or disprove what he had seen, or what Bernard had hinted at. It was a damp storage space. Soon to be demolished and forgotten.

Jack stepped back out into the corridor and pulled the door of the room closed.

After four steps along the corridor Jack stopped and looked back at the closed door. He had the distinct, but unexplainable feeling that someone had just called his name. Almost akin to hearing your name in a busy shop and realising it was not you being addressed. Jack frowned. It wasn't just his name. It was the voice.

Jack went back to the door and turned the handle. The metal was cold. The door refused to move. He put both hands to the door and pushed. The wooden barrier remained immobile.

"Rats with a key," Jack said as he moved away from the door. He looked to his right, at the covered window. It may have been his imagination, he thought, but he would swear the blind was moving. As though it had just been dropped back into place.

12


After leaving her car in a slot outside a GP practice that stated Patient Parking Only, Frank walked around the corner into a side street parallel to one of the town centres main roads. It was a partly residential area, part small businesses. Most of them appeared to be under Polish or Middle Eastern management. Frank passed a group of men standing on a corner. They were in casual clothes, all barring one, bearded. None of them were speaking English. They watched Frank as she passed.

This is just stupid, Frank thought as she spotted the building she was looking for and stopped outside. The last time she had been here she had left feeling frustrated and mildly angry, in spite of the odd reassuring glow on her mother's face. Then she remembered Georgie and the blue-rinsed old lady in the supermarket. They were not suffering sleep deprivation. Absurd as she felt it was, Frank's main concern was the safety of Georgie. She had read enough books to remember that to establish the truth you had to eliminate the impossible.

And Conan-Doyle had been a believer.

The building appeared to have once been a small church, or chapel. Between two dirty gate posts, with no gate, a path led up to the front doors. They were arched and wide, made of dark wood, with heavy metal hinges. Above the doors, set in the large stones of the wall was a round window with dark, stained glass. It was covered by a protective screen of thick wire mesh.

"2nd Spiritualist Church," a sign affixed to the wall above the doors read.

"What happened to the first one?" Frank muttered as she turned to her right, following the advice of a sign, with a badly drawn arrow, that said, "Office."

Frank's search on her phone in Tesco's carpark had eventually provided her a number that had been answered by a woman called Carol Nuttall. Ignoring the implications of that surname, Frank had explained her recent experiences and been invited to call in.

"It's a more common experience than you may imagine," the woman had reassured Frank.

Frank pushed open a door into a side building attached to the church. It looked like a brick lean-to, added hastily, and without a lot of thought, to the older building. Inside, a small space held a row of cheap plastic chairs, poster covered walls and a desk.

"Hello, can I help you?" the woman sat behind the computer on the paper strewn desk was ten years Frank's senior. She was dressed in a smart pinstriped jacket over a cream blouse. Her sleekly straight blonde hair framed a face that could have just arrived from a demonstration session in Boots No 7 department.

Frank felt a little underdressed in her jeans, denim jacket and T shirt. Her own concession to daytime make-up generally involved a lathering of moisturiser, an application of mascara and, if totally necessary, a swipe of lippy. She felt like the poor relation coming for a handout.

"I called you earlier. About…" Frank's voice failed her. She was not sure what she had called about, to be honest.

"Mrs. Blake?" the woman stood behind her desk and extended a hand. "I'm Carol, Carol Nuttall. It was me you spoke to." She gave Frank a very white smile with unnaturally even teeth.

Frank nodded and returned the smile half-heartedly. "Miss," she corrected the woman. "Frank to most people."

"Would you like a coffee?" Carol asked.

Frank looked around the small reception area. It was a busy little space. The desk was littered with opened letters and sealed envelopes. Behind there were filing cabinets with a few drawers left half open, files laid across the top. On Frank's side of the desk the walls were decorated with leaflets and posters. Upcoming visits to the church by itinerant mediums were surrounded by contact numbers and business cards form people offering readings, aura interpretations and various forms of healing and fortune telling.

"You know what?" Frank said, trying to increase the wattage of her smile to match Carol's. "I think I may have got a bit ahead of myself. No coffee thanks. It's probably all stress. I haven't been sleeping well lately. I'm sorry. I probably shouldn't have bothered you."

"Your Aura says otherwise." The voice was light with an almost musical lilt.

Frank turned to face the man who had stepped into reception. He was tall, easily six feet, and very slim. He wore a tweed jacket over a denim shirt, buttoned to the neck, jeans and oxblood Doctor Marten boots. His thin face was adorned by a neatly trimmed, dark beard. Above his large pale eyes his eyebrows were finely arched. The hair on the sides and back of his head was shaved close to the scalp, but it was long enough on top to be tied in a top knot reminiscent of a samurai warrior.

"I'm Gavin Darcy," the man said, advancing on Frank. "I think I've met your mother...Sylvia?"

"You were lucky Gavin was here," Carol said. "That's why I suggested you call in."

"I was just explaining, I may have been mistaken," Frank said.

Gavin stood before Frank and placed one hand on his hip. He tilted his head to one side and made circular motions with his free hand. "I don't think so," he told Frank. "That healthy green Aura of yours has some nasty ripples around the edges. It has been disturbed." He dropped his hand and raised his eyebrows as he stared at Frank. "Recently?" he asked.

"Aura?" Frank asked quietly and looked at Carol.

"Gavin is a Sensitive," Carol offered in explanation. It was of little help to Frank.

"Carol mentioned some mumbo-jumbo about your house being haunted," he flapped his hand at Frank, dismissing the idea. "Whatever's been bugging you is not interested in house prices or interior décor."

"What do you mean?" Frank asked.

"Someone's been following you," Gavin said with a mock quiver in his voice as he wiggled his fingers.

The interior of the church had been altered drastically Frank guessed as she sat on a plastic chair and looked around. Where there had probably once been an altar the floor was raised into a stage. The seating area consisted of ranks of red chairs with black tubular frames. Not a pew to be seen. Overhead, beneath the original beams of the building's roof, fluorescent strip-lights were suspended to illuminate the space. Over the stage, a circular stained-glass window let in a little light through its dirty surface.

"Tell me what's happened," Gavin said, sitting near Frank, an empty seat between them. "And more importantly what you've felt."

Frank looked down and sighed. This all felt so stupid. Then she thought of Georgie. Whatever kept him safe, no matter how stupid it seemed, was worth a punt. She returned her gaze to Gavin and told her story.

While Frank talked Gavin kept his eyes on her, nodded and made small noncommittal sounds, like someone who had done a counselling course. When she finished he turned his attention to his fingers and fiddled with the obviously manicured nails.

"Do you suffer from panic attacks usually?" Gavin asked.

"Never," Frank said firmly.

"And your son didn't give much of a description," Gavin noted, still looking at his hands.

"No," Frank confirmed, "Georgie calls all older men Granddads."

Gavin nodded. "No one in the family is a pipe smoker, I'm guessing?"

"No."

Finally, Gavin raised his eyes and looked at Frank. "These things can be transient," he said. "Just something lost. Searching for something, as if in dream. Sleepwalking. The opening of the doors is very suggestive." He gave Frank a smile. "My best guess would be that it has gone now. Whatever attached itself to you has gone."

"How can you know that?" Frank asked.

Gavin stroked his beard before he answered. "We're alone here, Frank," he said. "I feel nothing. You experienced something at your work, in your car, at home, and in Tesco. The common denominator is you. Spirits, whatever you like to call them, they behave like this. They will attach themselves to someone, and when they don't find what they're looking for they..." he made a starburst gesture with his fingers, "Poof!" Gavin held his thumb up before him and studied the nail. "For me the Panic Attack is the nail in the coffin," he gave a small smile.

"The Panic Attack?"

"You are not an anxious person." It was a statement, not a question.

"Definitely not," Frank said.

"No," Gavin said. "And I'm pretty sure it wasn't your Panic Attack you were experiencing."

"The lady in Tesco said the old man turned and walked away," Frank said.

"Back to where he came from," Gavin nodded.

"The hospital."

Gavin stopped his examination of his cuticles and placed his hands on his thighs. He looked down at them for a moment before he returned his gaze to Frank's face. He suddenly seemed to find maintaining eye contact difficult and he looked at her then away towards the stage and the stained-glass window.

"Do you know Emily Greene?" he asked.

13

Just after the evening meal the alarms sounded, summoning staff assistance to the female half of the Harbour. The noise was a persistent beeping, not particularly loud, but penetrating. It was the third time it had sounded that day.

Jack stood in the corridor outside the patient lounge and watched two members of staff scuttle towards the dividing door, pulling at the keys attached to their belts as they moved. The man and woman disappeared and the door was pulled hurriedly shut, and locked, behind them.

Jack strolled to the office and knocked on the door. A young staff nurse, long hair in a ponytail, the regulation dark trousers and subdued, patterned top, opened the door.

"I want to get out for a walk," Jack said. "Walk off the gourmet, reheated stew."

"You pick your moments, Jack," the girl said to him. She swung her eyes over a large white board on the office wall. "Grounds only," she reminded him.

"Half an hour," Jack told her, "an hour, tops. I'll be back in time to finish working on my escape tunnel before bed."

The nurse laughed. She walked beside him along the short corridor to the ward door, key in hand.

Jack had been planning another visit to the storage room that had been on his mind most of the afternoon. When he stepped into the main corridor he revised that idea.

Outside the entrance to the female ward, three women were standing. One had her face pressed to the narrow window of the door while the others stood behind her.

"I bet it's her again," one of the women said. She was small with lank mousey hair. Her thin body shrouded in an oversized cardigan over T shirt and jeans.

"Maybe you got lucky, if they won't let you back in," Jack said as he stopped next to the women.

"They said we have to wait a minute," the thin woman said. She folded her arms and pulled her cardigan around her. "It's that lass," she added, "at it again."

The woman closest to the door kept her face pressed to the glass and ignored Jack. The third one, larger, with a flushed face, looked at him over the thin woman's head then turned her attention back to the door.

"I don't think I'd be clambering to get back in if they locked me out," Jack said. "Anyway, I'm off to the Rec hall, if anyone wants a coffee."

After a momentary hesitation the thin woman took the bait.

"Are you buying?" she asked. "My purse is in there." She pointed at the ward door.

"It's a date," Jack said and moved off with a nod of his head.

"You're Jack, aren't you?" The small woman fell into step beside Jack.

"I'm that famous?" Jack asked.

"One of the lasses on our ward fancies you. I'm Wendy. It's not me!" she added hurriedly.

"Wendy's a made-up name, you know?" Jack commented, ignoring the school yard banter.

"Made up," Wendy asked, "what you on about?"

"Barrie," Jack told her, "the guy who wrote Peter Pan. He made your name up."

"Barry?" Wendy frowned at him. The pale, thin skin of her forehead creased. "Barry who? Peter Pan's a cartoon, isn't it?"

Jack looked at her and was about to deliver a barb, but her earnest query caused him a pang of guilt when he thought about winding her up.

"I think your right," he said. "Let's get those coffees. They may have scones left."

"I hope so," Wendy agreed. "That pigging stew at teatime was disgusting. I chucked mine away."

"I think it was supposed to be lamb," Jack said as they arrived at the Recreation Hall.

The entrance to the Rec Hall was halfway along the long passageway, almost directly opposite the turning towards the hospital entrance. The room was the size of a church with a similarly shaped, beamed ceiling. At one end was a stage, concealed by heavy, dusty red curtains. The polished wood floor space held a scattering of tables and cheap, plastic seats. Assembled in front of a coffee shop set in a large recess, the chairs were occupied by a collection of patients and visitors. At the other end of the room from the stage were two full-sized snooker tables. The harsh clatter of the balls echoed above the chatter.

"Get a couple of seats and I'll get drinks," Jack said as they crossed the room.

Wendy nodded. "Big slice of cake," she said.

Jack looked at the clientele as he stood in a short queue at the counter. He thought about his daughter, living with Claire's parents. He had forbidden them from bringing her here to visit him. Three weeks was a long time for a child. And a father. But Jack knew it was for the best.

"What's going on on your ward?" Jack asked as he handed Wendy her coffee and cake and sat at the table. "Three times today that alarms gone off." His feigning of innocence was convincing.

"All sorts of queer stuff going on," Wendy said with a spray of lemon drizzle crumbs.

"You said it's that lass again," Jack quoted her.

Wendy took a swig of coffee, looking at Jack over the mug. "That Emily. Not always her, though," she told him, "she only come in a couple of days ago. But seems since then everyone's on edge. She doesn't help mind. Banging on about ghosts all day and half the night."

"What weird stuff?" Jack asked.

Wendy shook her head and held her cake in front of her face ready to bite. "Oh, stuff going missing then people fighting saying it's been taken. Someone's moving stuff and putting it in other people's bed areas. Arguments. Last night someone was banging a side-room door on and off all night. Then that stupid Karen woke up screaming she was on fire."

"So why the alarms all day?"

"Oh, there was a fight," Wendy said. "Over something getting moved. Then Emily tried to get off the ward twice." Wendy waved her arm dismissing all the nonsense. The sleeve of her large cardigan slid up to reveal a forearm that was a patchwork of scar tissue.

"She just wants to go home, like everyone else, I suppose," Jack commented.

"Who knows where she wants to be," Wendy said. "Last time she was screaming The Angel's calling her."

"Angels," Jack echoed with a frown.

Wendy finished her cake. "Hey, she's dead strong though. She pushed people out the way when the door was open and shot off the ward."

"Did she get far?"

"Nah," Wendy shook her head and laughed. "Went the wrong way. She only made it down the back corridor before they jumped on her."

Jack drank the last of his coffee and put the mug on the table.

14

Frank sat on the edge of her son's bed and closed the book cover on the last page of The Enormous Turnip.

"That Granddad's not coming tonight," Georgie said. His eyes were huge, fastened on Frank.

"Nope!" Frank said firmly. "Just a dream. All gone."

Georgie yawned.

"You go to sleep," Frank said. "I'll just be in my room, reading my book."

"Is it about the big, tall soldier?" He enjoyed hearing the highlights of whatever Frank was reading.

Frank smiled. "No," she told him. "This one's about the girl whose soppy boyfriend ran away."

"Like Daddy," Georgie noted.

"He didn't run away from you," Frank said. Just me, she thought. To be with his bottle-blonde temp. "Now, sleep time. Remember I'm going to work in the morning, so, up early."

Georgie rolled over and held a hand up above his head. Frank high-fived him. Their new ritual. She watched him close his eyes and snuggle into his pillow. It felt as if there was no room in her heart for anyone else.

On her bed Frank opened her book, read half a page she had read before, and dropped it beside her. She sighed.

Why had she agreed to work an extra shift tomorrow, when she could have had a whole day off? Overtime, extra money? Or because she was a soft touch and had bought into Angela's desperation on the phone? Two people on the female ward had called in sick. The ward was struggling. Partly because of Emily Greene.

Which made Frank think about Gavin Darcy.

Frank had sidestepped Gavin's question about Emily. She could not talk about a patient in hospital. To anyone. Gavin had told her he understood. He was a friend of Emily's mother. She and Emily had attended the church regularly. Mrs Greene, and quite a few other people, believed that Emily was a particularly gifted psychic. But at only nineteen it was a gift that Emily had barely begun to understand, let alone control. She was like a radio receiver with no ability to tune in or adjust the volume, Gavin stated. The situation was made worse by Emily's mother's estranged husband. He had no belief, and even less tolerance. Mental Health Services and Social Services, bound by common sense, sided with Mr Greene. If Emily was so distracted she could not sleep, neglected to eat, and had dropped out of college, there really was only one place she could find help.

Frank put her book on the bedside cabinet and turned back her duvet. It was early, but she was tired, and had already locked up downstairs and felt ready to sleep. She gave a half smile as she moved the Louisville Slugger and rolled it under her side of the bed.

Which made her think of Gavin again.

In spite of common sense Frank had been reassured by the odd man's calm voice and matter of fact explanation of her experiences. Perhaps she had needed a little strangeness to refocus her own sensibilities. Get things in perspective. She had been tired, over wrought, and experienced a panic attack. Whether that was her reaching the end of her tether with nonsense or, as was Gavin's view, the projected feelings of a spirit overwhelmed by the world beyond its usual experience, she did not know. The important thing was she returned home feeling reassured and relaxed. To a house devoid of odd smells, where the big fire engine remained on top of the overflowing toybox.

Frank felt a little guilty about Gavin. He had helped her, somehow. And she had closed down his enquiry about Emily. He may have just wanted to ask how she was. His explanation of how he knew her had faltered, then shattered, against Frank's shield of confidentiality.

Frank turned the bedside radio on. She slipped beneath her duvet as some inane warbling about Prehistoric French Cave Art on Radio 4 lulled her towards sleep.

The sound of screaming woke her.

She rolled over on the stiff mattress of the single bed and coughed. She could smell smoke. Looking up she saw that the ceiling was hidden by a thin layer of billowing, grey gas.

Fire!

She stood and felt a wave of exhaustion, or was it the smoke, sap her strength. She was tired. Surely, she had only been in bed minutes, an hour at most, after a long shift, then pressing and starching her apron and cap for tomorrow.

Starching? Frank registered the strange thought.

On the landing girls were running, calling to each other. Most were in night dresses, a few in uniforms with white aprons and stiff, erect caps. Smoke crept along the ceiling and sent delicate, insidious fingers into the air. At the far end of the landing, the stairwell, the smoke was thicker, illuminated by a flickering orange glare. The air, beneath the roiling ceiling was warm and stuffy.

"We are trapped," a girl screamed close to her. "The stairs are aflame!"

Panic swept over her and she turned back and forth, unsure where to go. Girls passed going each way, frantic, aimless like flies in a glasshouse. The screams increased in frequency and volume. A figure emerged from a room close to the stairwell encased in flame. Her screams were piercing and heartrending.

This way.

It was not a voice. It was something in Frank's head. Louder than a whisper.

Turning away from the increasingly ferocious glow and escalating heat she faced the darkness. And froze.

In the shadows something beckoned. Dark, shrouded, with burning eyes, it called to her. As it reached out to her the darkness swelled behind it, the outstretched arms like the wings of the Angel of Death.

She screamed, turned, and ran into the flames.

"Jesus!" Frank sat bolt upright in bed seconds before the alarm began to sound.

## 15

Jack woke during the night again.

This time he had no doubts about what had woken him. It was not Mark Pickering. Unless his nocturnal activities had taken a new turn. Somewhere, someone was hammering on a door.

Jack stood and went through the ritual of straightening his T shirt and shorts then walked out from his curtained sleeping quarters. The dormitory was in half-darkness as usual. Other men were stirring from their beds. There was the sound of muttering and hushed voices raised in query.

"The hell's going on?" Mark's head appeared through the gap in his bed curtains.

Jack ignored him and pushed open the dorm door. The sound, a heavy fist or a boot banging against wood, stopped abruptly.

Jack watched as two staff members walked away from him. They went down the corridor, passed the small toilet beyond the side-rooms and stood looking at the last door. It was closed, a square window set in the top quarter. Behind it there was a stairwell that only the staff used, and then rarely. It led to the side entrance of the High Dependency Unit on the ground floor, as far as Jack recalled. Early in his admission he had prowled the ward looking for points if egress in earnest.

Men in various states of undress appeared from rooms and followed Jack's gaze as he watched the staff, who stood before the closed door in quiet conversation. The staff nurse, a young woman called Claire, looked back down the corridor towards her disturbed patients. Ben Shelton stepped around her and unlocked the door and swung it open.

Claire looked at the dark opening revealed inside the doorway and stepped away from it. She looked towards Jack again. "Something loose, banging in the wind," she sounded unconvincing. The expression on her face even less so.

Jack walked towards her as Ben leant into the opening. The soft, repeated clicking of a light switch sounded. The darkness inside the opening remained. Ben grunted.

"Just close it, Ben," Claire said. There was an odd tone in her voice.

The tall nursing assistant closed and locked the door. He shrugged his shoulders.

"Okay, let's try getting back to bed," Claire said as she moved away from the door.

Jack turned and found himself almost face to face with Bernard. The little man, in his checked pyjamas, looked up at Jack and raised his eyebrows quizzically.

"Which one of you thieving gits has got my watch?" Mark's voice came loudly from the dormitory.

"I'll ring downstairs and make sure that staircase is locked at their end," Claire said to Ben as they passed Jack.

After breakfast Jack sat in the dayroom. With a review with the consultant planned he was tied to the ward for the morning. In a corner chair with his back to a window and a dull, grey morning, he flicked over the pages of a newspaper. It kept his hands occupied. His thoughts were elsewhere.

On his bed, after the disturbance during the night, Jack had listened to the sounds of the other patients returning to their beds. The few muttered exchanges he overheard echoed his own opinion. The knocking on that door had been no more the wind than it had been the Tooth Fairy. The expression on the nurse's face had told him she knew the same. He thought about his conversation with Wendy. He wondered what was going on in the old building. And if everything was connected.

Eventually he had to force himself to relax and change his line of thought. He did not want to be led astray by a bunch of excited, over-firing braincells. When he drifted off he was hoping the hum he could hear was just the background sound of the world turning, and not inside his head.

Jack looked up from the paper he was not reading when the overhead lights flickered and died. The other men sitting around the room stopped talking and turned their heads. The large room became dim, illuminated only by the weak daylight entering the windows.

"Anyone got a shilling for the meter," one of the older men in the room said.

Across the room from Jack, anchored firmly in a sturdy cabinet, and in spite of the apparent lack of power, the TV suddenly came to life. The screen lit up with a bright display of swirling snow, gave a sudden loud hiss of static, then died as quickly as it had flared up.

There was a metallic clatter as something fell and bounced across the floor in the ward kitchen, next door to the lounge. A female scream followed this, then the sound of crockery smashing.

Jack dropped the paper on the seat beside him and stood up. He took a step towards the open doorway to the corridor.

"Don't!" The voice stopped Jack in his tracks.

In the opposite corner to where Jack had been sitting a young man was standing. He had one arm extended towards Jack, the fingers spread on his trembling hand. Tall and thin the man wore a baggy sweatshirt over baggier jeans. His feet were bare. His eyes, in a pale face surrounded by long, lank hair, were fastened on Jack. His name was Tom, or Tim, Jack registered. One of those young lads who had addled his brain with drugs and spent long hours gazing into space with silently moving lips.

"Just a power cut," Jack said. "I was going to see if-"

"Don't go out there yet," the young man said and took a couple of steps forward like a malfunctioning robot. "Let them pass. Just let them go by."

Jack looked at the doorway. Apart from two members of staff approaching from the office the corridor was empty. The sound of something hitting the floor made Jack frown and turn his head.

Tom, or Tim, was face down on the thin nylon carpet. His limbs jerked as he convulsed. Soft grunts accompanied his loud, uneven breathing.

The ceiling lights sparked back on and the insistent beeping of the alarm system cut into the silence that had engulfed the ward.

## 16

Frank got out of her car in the hospital carpark. It was barely light, a water colour streak of pale yellow cloud away in the east. The air was cold and damp. Pulling the fur trim of her parka hood closer to her neck she crossed the rough ground of the parking area. She looked to her right where a stationary, huge yellow machine, that would have fascinated Georgie, stood guard over a pile of rubble a couple of hundred metres away.

Frank remembered her dream.

The mound of shattered brickwork and disturbed earth was all that remained of a two- storey building that had most recently been a centre for young people. Before that, long ago, it had been the on-site residences for some of the nursing staff. Its claim to infamy was being the site of a fire that had taken the lives of a number of the young women living there.

I should not have agreed to do this shift, Frank thought. The place was getting into her head. She could hear her mother's disapproving voice in her mind. Nightmares. Believing in ghosts. A panic attack. Turning to a spiritualist church for help. For God's sake! What was she thinking? Was she ill?

Depressed? Was all this the backlash from the break-up with Pete?

"I tell you, the place is alive with rats!" Two porters were having a heated discussion as Frank walked through reception. "You can hear them scratching. Scattering stuff around down that back, bloody corridor all night." The speaker was pulling a coat on, preparing to leave.

"It's closing the wards. No food. They're looking for somewhere else to live." The porter taking over the day shift flicked on the lights in the small office. "They'll be queuing up for meals with the patients next," he told his mate.

Frank trudged down the corridor avoiding making eye contact with those coming and going, still deep in thought. She was not looking forward to standing through a handover about almost thirty women she knew nothing about, and a shift on a ward with enough variations in routine to make her feel like a fifth wheel. She hoped Joyce was working. One sensible nursing assistant could turn the tide on a shift that would otherwise descend into chaos and aggravation.

"I wouldn't have been here," Joyce said, to Frank's relief, after the handover, "if I hadn't had to change a shift. Brian has a scan on Thursday and I needed to swap."

Frank felt a little pang of guilt. Joyce's husbands recent battle with cancer had played to her advantage. "How is he?" she asked.

"He's doing OK, Frances," Joyce said. "If this scan is clear, we're on the home straight. He's frightened of course, but there's always hope."

"Good," Frank said. They were standing just outside the office door and she looked back into the room. Two young women were sitting engrossed in the screen of a mobile phone while the staff nurse from the night shift stood over them, frowning as she shrugged herself into her coat.

"I'll shift those two along," Joyce said, indicating the two girls. "Start getting everyone up and about." She smiled at Frank. "You do what you need to do, then I'll do the meds with you after breakfast."

"Thanks, Joyce," Frank said.

Joyce stepped back into the office. "Right, you two," she said, "unless we're going to rouse these ladies via Facebook we better have a walk around the ward. Don't you think?"

Frank wandered the upper floor as Joyce organised the other nursing assistants, Amanda and Dawn, into giving the patients their morning call and assisting or cajoling those who needed help or reminders about hygiene.

Like her own ward, the female habitat was showing signs of aging and the need for redecoration. The magnolia walls were scuffed in places, doors were scratched and marked and the toilets and wash area cold in spite of the ancient chunky radiators.

Frank stepped to one side of the passageway as an irregular progression of women began to wander back and forth from the dorms, side-rooms and washrooms.

"Probably best to leave Emily asleep," Joyce said, coming up behind Frank. "You could leave Amanda or Dawn up here until after breakfast and we can get her up after medication."

"She's finally sleeping?" Frank asked.

Joyce raised the eyebrows of her open, friendly face. "They finally zonked her with a concoction of meds," she said.

"Which room?"

Joyce pointed and Frank went and stood in the open doorway before entering.

Emily was curled up under a yellow blanket on top of the bed. In almost a foetal position, all that was visible was her face and her hair, fanned across the pillow like a dark halo. Frank stood beside the bed and looked at her. She looked far younger than her nineteen years.

"Looks like butter wouldn't melt. Doesn't she?" Joyce said from the doorway.

"Hard work?" Frank said.

Joyce sighed. "It's not just that, Frances," she said.

"What do you mean?" Frank frowned.

Joyce shook her head. "Half the patients, and some of the staff, are starting to be drawn in by her. If it was a hundred years ago they'd be talking about witches, ducking stools or burning her."

"What do you think?"

"She needs help." Joyce entwined her fingers and put her knuckles to her mouth. "Not my job to diagnose."

"Has her Mum been in to see her?" Frank asked, thinking of Gavin Darcy.

"Not allowed." Joyce shook her head again. "Some pact between Dad and Social Services. Mum is no longer next of kin. Officially."

They were interrupted by raised voices from one of the dormitories. Joyce looked down the corridor.

"Another argument," she said. "One of our ladies seems to be having fun winding everyone up moving their stuff around lately."

Frank stood in the doorway of Emily's room and watched Joyce bustle down the passage.

With breakfast squared away Frank plodded through the morning medication round, careful to check she was giving the right meds to the correct, unfamiliar patients. The women awaiting their pills and potions milled around the dayroom and the main ground-floor corridor. Frank and Joyce stood behind the wheeled metal cabinet on the edge of the dayroom.

Halfway through the process the persistent chirruping of the alarm system sounded.

Amanda came rushing out of the office, where a small wall panel displayed the origin of the alarm call. "Next door!" she called as she locked the office hurriedly. She jogged down the corridor towards the connecting door to the male ward.

"Makes a change," Joyce said. "We've had more than enough the last day or two with Emily and fights, and the electrics playing up, setting it off."

When Frank reached the top of the stairs, carrying Emily's morning meds and a small beaker of water, she was surprised to find Dawn standing near the small night office. From somewhere down the ward there was a repetitive thudding sound.

"Why are you down here?" Frank asked. "Where's Emily, and what's that flipping banging?"

The girl looked at Frank anxiously. She was short, soft looking and round. She had long dark hair in a ponytail and eyebrows that were very carefully shaped and coloured.

120

"She's in her room, still asleep." Dawn turned her eyes to the corridor. "It's a side-room door banging. I had a look, but there's no one there." She returned her gaze to Frank. Her eyes were very large and looked moist.

"Is there a window open?" Frank started towards Emily's room.

"No," Dawn answered in a quiet voice. She made no attempt to accompany Frank.

Frank gave the girl a scowl and walked on.

A few steps from Emily's open door the banging stopped. Frank gave the corridor ahead a curious glance then walked into the room.

Emily was sitting up, her legs bent, but still under the blanket. Her arms were wrapped around her shins and her forehead resting on her knees. Behind her bed a tall window showed an uninterrupted field of grey cloud. She did not look up as Frank entered.

"Lanky Frankie," Emily said, her voice muffled by the blanket and her legs.

Frank put the medication and beaker down on the small set of drawers beside the bed. She stood and looked at the girl.

Frank had been named by her father because of his lifelong admiration for Frank Sinatra. When she had been growing up she had gone through a pre-teen phase when she was all long limbs and angles. Teasing her at times her Dad had called her Lanky Frankie. No one else ever called her that. Just her Dad.

He had died three years ago.

## 17

Two weeks earlier Jack would not have been able to hold his tongue when confronted with Doctor Cornelius Giles, Consultant Psychiatrist. However, a fortnight back on his regular medication regime had at least re-established some of Jack's control over his mind to mouth reflex responses. The edge of his tongue was still sharp, but he was able to be selective and vent his frustration on appropriate targets. So sparing Dr. Giles, red-haired with bilateral hearing aids and prone to the occasional misinterpretation in his usually expert lip-reading, from the full force of Jack's cutting observations.

"Sit down, Jack, sit down." Giles waved to a seat in the small meeting room as Jack entered.

Jack sat on a low, cloth upholstered chair and looked around the room. Wooden armed chairs arranged in a rough circle, the standard hospital bland walls and neutral nylon carpet. A window behind Jack's seat looked out onto the field, carpark and the road beyond. The others in the room watched Jack as he settled in the chair.

Jenny Davis, tall, long dark hair and a pale face. Jack's community nurse. She nodded and smiled at Jack.

Dr Shah. Giles' junior. A small man with a bright smile and a closely cropped beard and head. He raised a hand in greeting. He had felt the force of Jack's venom recently. Jack was a little shamed, and relieved that the little man had not seemed to understand his asking if the doctor had been harmed when he had fallen off the side of the jar of jam.

The final member of what Jack thought of as The Parole Board was a staff nurse from the ward. Jess looked very young, was slightly over-weight, but pleasantly rounded, and had a raucous laugh when she unleashed it.

"How's the world treating you, Jack?" Giles asked and smiled. They were old sparring partners, each aware of the other's foibles and views.

"I'll be better when you autograph that form rescinding my section," Jack answered.

Giles looked at Jack over the top of his spectacles. "All in good time, as you well know, Jack." He raised one eyebrow. "Let's try and avoid you knocking out anymore Vicars."

Jack relaxed back into his chair and gave a half smile. "A tad extreme, I'll admit," he said. "Anyway, it was a slap. I wasn't charged."

"Because I intervened with the police," Giles said. He looked at Dr Shah sitting beside him and pointed to Jack's medication chart on the smaller man's knee. "Meds seem to be doing their job again." He said before returning his eyes to Jack. "Now that you're taking them."

"Different circumstances." Jenny spoke up in Jack's defence. "We know Claire's illness put a lot of stress on Jack."

Giles nodded his head. "Of course," he said. "You still have a lot to deal with," he told Jack. "That's why I'm sitting on you. It's not for my own amusement, Jack."

Jack had nothing to say. He was thinking about Claire.

"Have you seen your daughter?" Jenny asked Jack.

"What?" Giles said before Jack could respond.

"I asked-" Jenny said, but Giles cut her short.

"What did you say?" Giles turned to Dr Shah and raised a hand to his ear.

"I did not speak," Dr Shah looked puzzled.

Jenny frowned. "She's with Claire's parents?" she confirmed.

"What!" Giles said again in a slightly exasperated tone.

Dr Shah frowned.

"What is it you want to know?" Giles asked his assistant. His voice had an edge to it.

"I did not speak anything," the little man repeated.

Jack, Jenny and Jess looked at the two doctors as Giles turned in his seat to face Shah.

"I distinctly heard you…" Giles voice failed him and he lifted both hands to his ears. His fingers moved over the hearing aids. He tilted his head, clearly listening to something.

"Is everything alright, Dr Giles?" Jess asked.

Giles looked around the room, his expression confused. "Erm, yes," he answered hesitantly. "There isn't an induction loop on the ward?" he asked Jess.

She mirrored his confusion and said, "What's that? No…no!"

"Strange," Giles murmured. "Something odd. I'm picking up some sort of interference. A voice."

"You can get tablets for that," Jack said drily.

Giles ignored Jack. "No one else hears it?" he asked.

"What?" Jenny said.

"A voice," Giles said again. "Asking the same question. Repeating."

"Asking what?" Jess said.

"Do you know?" Giles answered. "Just that, 'Do you Know?'"

Jack rubbed the back of his hand across his chin. "No one knows," he said, but no one heard him because of the knocking on the door.

## 18

Frank sat on the end of the bed and looked at Emily. The girl remained motionless, head on her knees. She said nothing else.

"Emily," Frank asked, "why did you call me that?"

Emily raised her head. Dark hair framed her small face, a few errant strands hanging forward. Her eyes were dull and half closed. "What?" she asked.

"You called me Lanky Frankie," Frank explained. "Why did you call me that?"

"I dunno," she began to lower her head again. "Heard it," she murmured. Her legs sank below the blanket as though she were deflating. She lowered her head to the pillow and closed her eyes.

"Emily!" Frank stood and shook the girls shoulder. There was no response save a soft guttural snore.

Frank looked at the beaker and medication on the drawers. It could wait, she decided.

As she stood looking down at the bed the banging noise started up again from the corridor.

"Dawn!" Frank stood in the doorway of the side-room and called to the nursing assistant.

There was no answer.

The corridor was empty in both directions. The sound was coming from Frank's left, beyond the T junction. The opposite direction to the office and the stairs to the lower floor. She looked back at Emily reclined on the bed and then set off towards the sound. Emily was not the only patient who had been left upstairs Frank guessed.

Three doors to the right, at the head of the T junction, Frank could see the cause of the sound. One of the side-room doors was opening and closing repeatedly about six inches. Each time it opened Frank could see a slice of the room. The foot of the bed and a strip of pale yellow wall.

"Hello," Frank said and stopped outside the room. "What's all that noise for?"

The door closed with a harder and louder slam making Frank step back in surprise. Then it swung slowly open allowing Frank a view of the whole room.

Bed, wardrobe, drawers. A window with a view of the grey sky above the roofline of the rear part of the hospital.

Frank uttered a short expletive and stepped further back until she bumped into the wall behind her.

The room was empty.

Frank's heart skipped a beat then accelerated. She looked up and down the corridor and suddenly experienced the same illusion she had in Tesco. The passageway seemed to sweep away in both directions. She pulled at the loose, round neck of her top, feeling a tightness in her throat. Still with her back to the wall she side stepped away from the open door of the empty room. Willing herself to calm down Frank took as deep a breath as she could manage and closed her eyes.

Something moved in front of her and Frank opened her eyes. She focused on a dark shape in the doorway of the side room. It disappeared inside.

"Are you alright, Frances?" Joyce asked as she emerged and closed the door behind her. "You look even paler than usual," she smiled.

"The door was banging," Frank said shakily as she gave a weak smile. Her heart was slowing. The tightness in her neck receding.

"Oh, they do that all the time," Joyce said and patted Frank's shoulder. "Draughts, faulty old locks and hinges. The slightest thing sets them off." She smiled and gently turned Frank away from the room, back towards Emily. "And the ghosts, of course," she added.

"Ghosts?" Frank asked.

"If you believe the likes of Dawn and Amanda," Joyce laughed. "Dawn came running downstairs as if she'd just seen one."

"Can we take Emily downstairs?" Frank did not want the girl left unattended.

"I'll sort her," Joyce said. "You go down. Have a cup of tea. We'll be down shortly."

They reached Emily's room and stopped outside. The girl was still on the bed, eyes closed.

"Sure?" Frank asked.

"Go," Joyce said. "You need to keep an eye on the Chuckle Sisters."

Frank laughed. The panic had passed completely. She thanked Joyce and turned away, heading for the stairs. Halfway there she stopped suddenly. She had left the medication in the room. She did not want Emily to have it just yet. Whatever her mental state, she was clearly over sedated at the moment. Frank needed to speak to the on-call medic if Emily was not more awake when she arrived downstairs.

Frank re-entered the passageway to the dorms and side rooms and paused as she heard voices. Emily and Joyce were talking.

"Shush," Joyce said, "it's alright. They won't while I'm here."

"That nurse. Frankie?" Emily's small voice was low but audible.

"Frances?" Joyce queried.

"Frances," Emily echoed. "She was here the other night. I wanted to tell her, but I was scared."

"Tell her what, Honey?" Joyce's voice was very soft.

"One was following her," Emily said. "An old man."

Frank's heart resumed its hammering. She took a long, silent breath through her open mouth.

"Alright." Joyce's voice became a little firmer. "Enough now. Let's get up and washed."

"I couldn't tell her," Emily sounded close to tears. "Every time I try to explain they give me more drugs. Keep me here. I can't get away." She paused and took a shaky breath. "So many of them. All afraid. I…" she stopped abruptly.

"You what, Hun?" Joyce asked.

"She's still here," Emily said.

"Who?"

"Frances," the girl said.

Frank turned and walked to the stairs. She did not look back or stop to lock the door behind her.

## 19

Everyone in the small meeting room looked towards the door as it swung open.

"I'm sorry to interrupt, Dr Giles." Staff Nurse Alison Pink was thirty-something, slim with shoulder length fair hair and a pinched expression. Jack detected a tremor in her voice and thought she looked nervous.

Giles lowered a hand from his ear. "What's the problem, nurse?" he asked.

Alison gave Jack a quick glance and chewed her lip before answering. "Could you just come out onto the ward a moment," she said. "We have a bit of a problem."

"I think Dr Shah will be able to help you," Giles said dismissively. He frowned as his right hand drifted back to the side of his head.

Alison shook her head. "No. You please, Dr Giles," she said firmly.

"What's happening, Ali?" Jess asked, rising from her seat.

Alison stood with one hand on the door and looked over her shoulder. "I don't know," she said.

Giles sighed and stood up. He went to the door and followed Alison into the corridor trailed by Jess.

"I think maybe we should just wait here, Jack," Jenny Davis said as Jack stood.

Jack took two steps outside the room and stopped dead in his tracks. He clenched his fists at his sides and turned his head, squeezing his eyes shut. Like a sudden starburst his mind erupted with thoughts. Like a physical assault or a bellowing voice. He was swamped by images and words, sights and sounds. As though a metal bucket containing every memory he had every kept had been viciously kicked over. He grunted and staggered back a step.

Then it was gone. As quickly as it had emerged.

Jack felt that familiar buzz in the back of his head. A gear wheel spinning, threatening to leap out of control. He took a breath and unclenched his hands. Opening his eyes he looked down the corridor towards the lounge.

Giles and Alison were standing halfway down the passageway, outside the door to the staff office. Giles looked perplexed as he swung his head back and forth. Along the corridor, and in the dayroom, people were standing frozen in place. Hands at their sides, unmoving, each figure was facing in the same direction. Not everyone though, and not just men. A few patients were walking slowly among the dozen or more still figures, and Jess to one side of Giles and Alison had assumed the same static position.

"What's going on, Dr Giles?" Alison asked.

Giles opened his mouth as he gazed around him then closed it again.

Jack moved down the corridor. He looked at the first frozen man he came to. It was Bernard. The little man's eyes stared straight through Jack. He was not quite still Jack noticed. His lips were moving very slightly though no sound was audible.

"Bernard." Jack poked the smaller man in the chest with his finger.

Bernard rocked back a fraction but gave no sign that he saw or heard Jack.

"Some sort of catatonic state." Jack looked over his shoulder to find Giles behind him.

"What the hell have you been giving these boys, Doc?" It was the older man who had quipped about a shilling for the meter earlier. He was strolling along the corridor gazing into the faces of his fellow patients.

Jack took hold of Bernard's shoulders and shook him gently. "Bernard!" he said again loudly. There was no response.

"Mass hysteria?" Giles asked himself quietly.

"What happened?" Jack asked Alison.

"Nothing," she replied. "One of them stood up then a few more. Nothing was happening."

Jack suddenly registered the dimness in the corridor. The muted daylight from the windows the sole illumination. "When did the lights go out again?" he asked.

"Couple of minutes ago," Alison told him. "Just here in the corridor and the dayroom. Just the trip switch." She frowned.

"I think you should go back and wait in the meeting room," Giles said to Jack.

Jack looked back towards the room. Jenny and Dr Shah were in the corridor. Jenny was returning Jack's gaze with a worried, quizzical expression. Shah was standing, hands at his side, in the same attitude as the rest of the frozen population of the ward.

"What the hell are they looking at?" Jack asked. He turned to face the same direction the static people where. What's there? he wondered. Toilets. The interior courtyard of the hospital. The back of the hospital.

Jack uttered a short explosive expletive. "The back corridor," he said.

"What-?" Giles began and stopped, looking over Jack's shoulder.

Jack turned to find that each of the frozen figures had turned their heads and were looking directly at him and Dr Giles. In unison they all took a breath and asked the same question.

"Do you know?"

A couple of seconds after Alison yanked the alarm fob from her belt the shrill beeping of the warning system filled the air.

20

Early in her nursing career, when she was a second-year student nurse, Frank had been given some advice by an aging ward sister who was rapidly approaching retirement. The advice had been offered as part of a less than thinly veiled attempt to recruit Frank into the ranks of a particular group of women who, at that time, were establishing a power base among the hospital middle management. Not being that way inclined Frank had sidestepped the advance and politely acknowledged the advice. However, she had remembered the words of wisdom. She kept them as almost a personal mantra to remind herself of how not to behave. The advice had been: If you want to get on in nursing, don't spend too much time with the patients.

For Frank hiding in the office was what nurses should not do. Reading and firing off e-mails, committing policies to heart and brown-nosing the likes of John Lawless were anathema to her. Yet, after returning to the ground floor, shutting herself in the office was exactly what Frank had done.

Having quickly checked that Amanda and Dawn were circulating among the patients Frank had retreated to the office, her heart still skipping unpleasantly along. She had logged into the computer and then sat staring at the screen with blank eyes. She had just experienced the second panic attack of her life, and more unsettling, overheard a conversation that made her question her own state of mind.

Frank swung her swivel chair around and turned her back on the computer screen. The office was a replica of the one in her own half of the ward. A box of a room festooned with notice boards, leaflets and a whiteboard listing the ward patients. An L shaped desk filled two walls and one corner. Diagonally opposite were filing cabinets and a trio of low, wooden armed seats. It was all familiar. But Frank felt as though she had stepped out onto the surface of the moon.

An old man was following her, Emily had said. And, she's still here. How the hell did the girl know that?

Frank had never run from much in her life. A bellicose sheep once on a school trip to a petting zoo. But important things? Never. So why did she have the overwhelming urge to ring her Mum now?

"Screw this!" Frank stood up and kicked the computer chair under the desk. I'm either losing the plot, she thought, or something weird is going on. The only way she knew to decide which was to take a hold of it and shake the truth out. The surge of anger had a calming effect on her.

"Hey, you," a small, thin woman accosted Frank as she stepped out of the office. "I need to go out for fags. Those drips in the dayroom said I had to ask you." She had lank, mousey hair and was encased in a cardigan two sizes too large.

"Right," Frank said. "What's your name. I'm sorry, but you know this isn't my ward."

"Wendy," the woman answered. "I've got leave and I can come and go as I like."

Frank leant against the office door where she could see the whiteboard through the slit window.

"What's your surname, Wendy?" she asked.

Wendy told her and Frank's eyes scanned across the rows of boxes decorated with ticks and scrawled writing until she found the little woman's leave status.

"Yeah, OK, Wendy," Frank said. She walked beside the woman to the ward main door. "Shops. An hour," Frank said as she unlocked the door.

Frank walked back from the door and turned into the corridor leading to the dayroom. Dawn was walking towards her. She had pulled the key from the fob on her belt and was swinging it around on the extendable cord.

"Alright if I go off for a smoke," she said. It was not a question.

"No," Frank said.

"What?"

"Why did you leave Emily on her own?" Frank asked.

"Hey?" Dawn rolled her large, heavily mascara ringed eyes. "She was in her room. I was coming to tell you about the banging."

"Where is she now?"

"In the dayroom with Jo-" Dawn stopped speaking.

The alarm system was calling out for their attention.

Frank checked the phone sized monitor on her belt, between the bunch of keys and her alarm fob and door-key. It displayed the origin of the alarm call on a calculator like screen.

"Next door," she said to Dawn. "Your cigarette break can wait." She pointed to the ward connecting door.

Dawn swung away and began to trot towards the entrance to the male ward. Her muttered "Snotty Bitch" clearly audible to Frank.

The ward dayroom was almost another mirror image of Frank's own ward. The same large, high ceilinged room decorated in uninspiring magnolia, tall windows with ancient, thin, floral curtains. Even the non-functioning electric fire in the white surround was the same model. The women, of various ages, were also echoing the scene Frank usually looked over. A few were in conversation, others navel gazing, some staring blank eyed at the muted TV. Half a dozen turned their heads as Frank walked into the room.

Emily and Joyce were sitting directly beneath one of the tall windows, leafless trees stark against the pale grey sky outside. Emily was dressed in a pink T shirt and jeans. She was looking down, her face partially shrouded by the dark curtain of her hair. Joyce was looking at Frank. Her expression was unreadable.

"I flushed that tablet," Joyce said when Frank reached them. "I wasn't sure if you wanted her to have it."

Frank nodded, biting back what she really wanted to ask. "Fine," she said coolly. "I wanted to see how Emily was and maybe talk to her doctor." She sat in the vacant seat beside the girl.

"Amanda is down in the toilets," Joyce said. "There was an argument about a missing towel," she rolled her eyes and smiled. Everything is normal.

Frank gave Joyce a brief but hard look. Things were far from normal. "How are you feeling, Emily?" she asked.

The young woman turned her head and looked at Frank as though she were stupid. A cynical, half-smile on her face. Then her eyes roamed over Frank's face and her expression softened. "Where are the cottages?" she asked.

"Cottages?" Frank queried.

Behind Emily Joyce shook her head.

"Where the Angels are," Emily said.

"I don't understand," Frank said.

"And flowers," Emily said. Her face looked slack. Her eyes enormous in her small face.

"Frank!"

Frank looked towards the door where John Lawless had just called her name. She shared a brief glance with Joyce before she stood and walked towards him.

Lawless towered over Frank by a good six inches and was probably twice her weight, verging on twenty stones. His large upper body was covered by a white shirt and a dated, paisley patterned tie. His second chin lapped over the tight collar of the shirt. His pale eyes, in the ruddy face, beneath the thatch of carefully arranged brown hair, watched Frank approach with a tinge of impatience.

"What can I do for you, John?" Frank asked.

Lawless turned away, beckoning Frank to follow with a gesture of the head. "I need you to go next door and help out," he said without looking at Frank. "Give me your keys and I'll sit on here for a while."

Frank stopped walking just before they reached the office. "What's going on?" she asked.

"They need another nurse next door," he turned to face Frank. His face was glowing. Beads of perspiration on his forehead.

"You're a nurse," Frank said, "as well as the manager."

Lawless held his hand out. "Keys!" he said. "And just for once, Staff Nurse Blake, try not to question every decision I make."

If holding your tongue were a physical action Frank would have bitten hers in two. She unclipped the ward keys from her belt and dropped them into Lawless' outstretched palm. Before she turned away she gave him the same expression of contempt with which she had favoured her ex-husband, after finding him removing a red leather miniskirt from an over the hill tart.

## 21

Jack took a couple of unsteady steps backwards and rested his behind on the ledge of one of the corridor windows. The whirring reverberation in the back of his head receded slowly as he looked up and down the passageway.

Giles and Alison where standing swinging their heads, confused by the sight before them. After their mutual exclamation those members of the ward who had spoken had collapsed, slumping to the floor like the proverbial sacks of potatoes.

"Oh, good work, Doc!" It was the meter man. He stood among the fallen bodies and ran a hand over his unshaven chin. "Kill or cure, hey?"

"What on Earth is going on?" Jenny Davis stood beside Jack. She pushed her hair back behind her right ear and gave him a puzzled expression.

"You tell me," Jack said.

Giles knelt beside the fallen Bernard and pressed his fingers to the man's throat. The movement seemed to galvanise

Alison and she knelt at the side of Jess. One of the nursing assistants, Dan Stevens, emerged from the day room looking wide-eyed.

"Syncope?" Giles said to himself, a metre from Jack's feet, on the floor beside Bernard.

"What?" Jenny said.

"He thinks they fainted," Jack replied, giving the twisted, cynical version of his broad smile.

"Ali, what do you want me to do?" Dan called. His young, sparsely bearded face looked anxious.

Alison was shaking Jess' shoulder, she looked at Dan with dazed eyes. "Ah, yea, right," she stammered. "Do a head count. Make sure everyone is accounted for."

"That'll help," Jack said. He looked towards the connecting door to the female ward as a plump young woman appeared. She stopped after closing the door and looked around with her mouth open.

"Eee, what's going on here?" The new arrival asked.

"It's the cavalry," Jack said sarcastically. "We'll be safe now."

"Jack!" Jenny said in a warning tone then moved away and knelt beside the fallen Dr Shah.

Jack watched the surviving staff tending to the fallen and exchange puzzled glances with each other. I might be mad but I'm not stupid, he thought. Whatever was going on here was not because he had neglected to take his Lithium Carbonate for six weeks.

"You, Mr Trench. Dayroom now!"

Jack looked toward the advancing figure that had mispronounced his name. It was John Lawless the hospital manager. Jack gave the ponderous butterball a mock salute and sauntered down the corridor. Either side of him lay the poleaxed bodies of the fallen.

In the dayroom a couple of men were standing looking out into the corridor. Five others were prostrate on the floor, their limbs spread at ridiculous angles.

"I knew they were putting Largactil in the tea," the meter man said behind Jack.

Jack turned in time to see Dan Stevens and John Lawless pass each other. Stevens heading into the main corridor and Lawless towards the exit.

"This is more like the dawn raid on Fort Knox," Jack said.

"Connery was the best Bond," the older man replied. He had a round face, grey hair circling his balding scalp.

Jack swung his eyes across the room. The standing men, the outstretched, unconscious bodies. Something was missing. What was it?

"Ali, we're one short," Dan Stevens called in the corridor.

"Where's Mark Pickering?" Jack asked.

22

Frank closed the door behind her and stood looking at a scene that would not have been out of place on a battlefield.

Along the corridor floor the still bodies of six people lay while Alison, Dr Giles and Jenny Davis knelt among them. Ahead more fallen men where visible in the dayroom. A few patients stood around, moving their heads as they surveyed the area.

"They're all breathing, just unresponsive," Dr Giles said.

"What happened?" Frank asked. She stepped around Bernard and approached Alison.

"We don't know," Alison replied.

"Ambulance?" Frank asked.

"I've sent Dawn to call," Alison said. "She's in the office."

"What do you want me to do?" Frank sank to one knee beside Bernard.

"Three men are off the ward," Alison said. "We're one short. I think it's Mark Pickering. Dan said he went upstairs just before…"

"Where's Dan?" Frank looked around.

"Went to find him."

"I'll check." Frank stood and walked down the corridor.

Around the corner the passageway led to the main entrance of the ward and a door to the stairs. Jack Trent was standing with one hand on the door. He looked at Frank as she approached.

"You better wait in the dayroom, Jack," Frank said pulling her key free of the fob on her belt.

Frank opened the door and began to ascend the stairs. At the dog leg bend, halfway up, she looked back. She had not heard the door slam and lock behind her. Jack was half a dozen steps behind her. He gave her a lop-sided grin.

"I'm not good at waiting," he said.

Frank was about to order him back down when a shout sounded from somewhere above them. She ran the rest of the way.

The sound of raised voices guided Frank to the back of the ward. The side-rooms, night toilet and the stairs down to HDU. Behind her she could hear Jack's following steps.

"Just keep out of the way, Jack," Frank ordered as they reached the T junction. She turned left and stopped.

Down at the end of the corridor, close to the HDU staircase, Dan Stevens was scuttling backwards on his behind and hands away from Mark Pickering. Mark was standing, moving after the crawling nursing assistant with a stiff legged gait. He was holding a red fire extinguisher at chest height like a shield, or a weapon. His face was red and bloodied from nose to chin, his forehead lacerated above his wide eyes. Above his dark jeans his T shirt was dotted with splashes of scarlet.

"Mark, Stop!" Frank called and walked forward slowly.

Mark shifted his gaze from Dan and the young man twisted onto his knees and shuffled quickly towards Frank and Jack.

"Get away!" Mark shouted. He raised the heavy red cylinder to his chin.

"Dan, get up before he throws that bloody extinguisher," Jack said.

153

Dan cast a quick look over his shoulder and pushed himself up, he skipped more than ran to join Jack beside Frank.

"Why is he bleeding?" Frank asked.

Mark turned back to the closed door of the staircase, the extinguisher swung against his thigh, his hand clasping the handle. With a sudden cry he stepped up to the door and butted his head against the already starred glass of the reinforced window at the top.

"That!" Dan said and pointed.

"Sound the alarm," Jack said

"I did," Dan pointed down the corridor. The white plastic fob of his alarm lay on the floor. "Nothing happened. He knocked me over."

"We need to stop him," Frank said. She moved forward again.

"He's six feet two and built like a brick outhouse," Jack said in warning.

"He's going to hurt himself," Frank shot Jack a fierce glare.

"Get out of my head!" Mark screamed and began a further onslaught against the window with his head.

"Enough!" Frank's shout seemed too loud for her slim frame. "Mark, stop!" she moved within six feet of the huge, blood splattered man.

"Bugger!" Jack pushed Dan forward. The younger, bearded man gave him an anxious glance. "Come on," Jack urged him.

"Mark!" Frank called again as Jack and Dan reached her.

Mark continued to batter the door with his head. The glass in the small window was shattered, held together by the wire reinforcing it inside. The door and window surround where smeared with blood.

"Hey, Pickering," Jack shouted. "You never heard of using a key?"

At the sound of Jack's voice Mark swung around. He glared at them and grimaced. His bared teeth were red with blood. He swung the arm holding the extinguisher behind him. The bear-like growl he emitted was appropriate to his dark, brooding appearance.

Jack sidestepped quickly, knocking Dan against Frank, who stumbled against the wall. The fire extinguisher flew at them and hit the wall beside Jack. Fragments of plaster flew into the air then danced across the carpet as the cylinder bounced and rolled along the floor.

"Get away!" Mark screamed again as he turned back to the door.

"Dan!" Frank gave the young man a quick glance, nodded at Mark and moved in on the big man. "Jack, go get help!" she shouted.

Mark lashed out as Frank touched his arm. She ducked back and the large sweeping arm made Dan totter back. He tripped and fell back onto his bottom on the floor again. Frank put her hands against the wall at her back as Mark stepped forward, fists clenched. His breathing was loud and ragged.

"They won't stop!" Mark screamed in Frank's face. It was a harsh, hissing explosion between his red teeth. Sprayed spots of blood landed on Frank's top.

"Pickering!" Jack shouted as he stepped around Dan on the floor.

Mark turned on Jack. He stood legs astride, his hands ready to strike, fists the size of sledgehammer heads. His eyes looked glazed and wild.

Jack took a step forward and ended the confrontation the best way he could. He did what the staff could not.

Mark grunted and squeezed his eyes shut as Jack's foot landed solidly between his legs. He bent forward, then, like a tower collapsing, sank to his knees on the floor.

"Stay down, Big Guy," Jack said putting his hand on Mark's shoulder and pressing down.

"Jack!" Frank stared at him with a shocked expression.

"He'll thank me," Jack said, "when the swelling goes down."

## 23

Frank turned on the washing machine and took a long pull from her glass of red wine. She rested her hip against the kitchen counter and watched the machine whirr into action. If the hot wash did not remove Mark Pickering's blood from her top she would bin it. Taking another mouthful of wine she walked through the hall and into the living-room. With a soft grunt she dropped onto the sofa.

The end of Frank's overtime shift had arrived before she had time to draw breath. The entry in Mark Pickering's electronic record had taken nearly an hour as she carefully worded her report. She had acknowledged Jack Trent's part in helping to stop Mark self-harming, but omitted how that had been achieved by a swift kick to the nuts. There was bound to be a Serious Untoward Incident investigation, but the SUI people could make their own minds up about how exactly Jack had saved Frank from an assault by a seriously disturbed patient.

If that is what had been going on.

Frank smiled as she thought about Jack. He was a tall, slim, cantankerous and moody individual on a good day. His lop-sided, often cynical grin, on a thin face topped by a thatch of unruly fair hair, never seemed to reach the blue eyes. It was there the sorrow in Jack's life was evident. Jack was a man life had kicked in the teeth. He was a bad tempered, gangly scarecrow with a chip on his shoulder. And because of that, maybe in spite of that, Frank liked him.

She could not say the same about John Lawless.

The routine demands of running an admission ward had prevented Frank from following up on the questions she had about Emily Greene. Medicine rounds, meals and the constant stream of requests from patients to leave the ward, go upstairs for forgotten items, telephone calls, PRN medication, who stole my watch, when is Dr Giles coming, she's wearing my socks, had swamped Frank.

The questions circulating in Frank's head were not about those things. Things she dealt with every day. They were about less concrete things. A girl who seemed to be seeing into her life. A girl who, if Gavin Darcy was right, was being denied the help she needed.

Frank's thoughts turned back to the rotund figure of John Lawless.

159

"Well you took your time." Lawless had swung the chair away from the computer screen when Frank returned to the ward. Behind him the monitor displayed a list of E-mails.

"They're waiting on an ambulance next door," Frank told him. "A lot of patients collapsed. One seriously self-harming. You should be over there."

"I have three people calling in sick," Lawless said. "Wards to staff. Things you do not ever have to worry about. And the duty doctor ringing here because you called them. What's that about?"

"Emily Greene is over sedated," Frank said.

"That girl is psychotic," Lawless said. "Her best interests are served by keeping her calm."

"To the point of unconsciousness?" Frank asked.

"I need this hospital under control while we transition to the new build," Lawless said.

"Even if we're not addressing the patient's needs?"

"You," Lawless stood up and stepped closer to Frank. He looked down at her. "You made a recent application to join the Crisis Team, I recall."

"And?" Frank queried.

"If you think I would sanction a transfer, or provide a reference to that band of know-it-alls, while you constantly undermine my authority, you have another think coming," Lawless stood close to Frank and looked down at her. "Emily Greene is psychotic. If you can't see that, then perhaps you're in the wrong job."

Frank looked at Lawless without speaking until he could no longer maintain eye contact.

"I know there is a faction on this ward who believe the girl," he had his back to Frank, tidying papers on the desk prior to leaving. "You are familiar with the term folie a deux?" He faced Frank again.

"I'm also familiar with the term duty of care," Frank replied.

Lawless gave her a cold stare as he walked out of the office and off the ward. All that remained was a faint, lingering trace of body odour.

Frank put her glass of wine down on the coffee table and looked up as a soft thud sounded above her head. For a split second she felt her heart flutter. She took a breath. There was no further sound. A toy falling from Georgie's bed, she decided.

At the foot of the stairs Frank thought about the panic attacks. They had been brief and so far had not returned. A hangover from her recent disturbed sleep was her best guess. She was not prone to anxiety and intended to remain that way. She went up to the landing.

The square at the top of the stairs was illuminated by the bathroom light, which she had left on. Around her the doors, apart from Georgie's, were closed. There had been no reoccurrence of the burning smell and no shadowy figures. She slid her head into the open gap of her son's room.

Georgie was mostly hidden by duvet. In the semi-dark of his room his fair hair looked almost dark on the pillow. His small, soft snores were clearly audible. On the floor beside his bed was a blue and yellow truck. He had held it in his hands when he got into bed. Frank withdrew her head and stood at the top of the stairs.

Ghosts. Was that really what was going on? No one had an explanation for what had happened at work. And Frank did not have one for what had happened in her home.

"Folie a deux," John Lawless had said.

The belief of others that the delusions of the mentally ill were a reality.

Frank walked down the stairs. In the living room she drained her glass. She looked around. A shelf of books. A blank TV. A tall, curved standard lamp. An ordinary place where extraordinary things did not happen. That would be madness. Frank knew she was not ill.

But she was starting to believe.

The sudden chirping of her mobile broke her thoughts. Frank scooped the phone up from the table and looked at the screen as she carried it and her glass back to the kitchen. After a moment's hesitation, her thumb hovering over the screen, she accepted the call and held the phone to her ear.

"Thanks for returning my call, Gavin," she said.

24

The next morning Jack was pacing the ward like a caged big cat. He could not settle in one place. Sitting in the dayroom listening to the muted background chatter, the rustle of newsprint and the clink of cups, had strained his patience as he tried to concentrate on the whirlwind of thoughts buffeting his mind.

He had woken early, disturbed by a dream. A nightmare in which he had been separated from Claire by an immense metal studded door. Although he had been able to hear her beyond the barrier he could not open the door or make his voice penetrate to Claire's side. Jack had returned to sudden consciousness with an unuttered scream on his lips expecting to see his hands bloodied and his fingernails cracked and shredded.

Jack measured the enormous L of the ground floor with strides as he covered the distance across the hard, beige carpet. From the main door, down the corridor. Passed the closed doors of the clinic, staff room and kitchen. Turning right, the entrance to the dayroom on his left, down towards the connecting door to the female ward. To one side the tall windows looked across the carpark, the field. To the other the office, two staff members laughing behind the slightly discoloured shield of laminated glass. Passed a spur corridor, narrow and windowless, leading to toilets and a laundry area. He stopped with his nose inches from the connecting door.

The girl, Emily Greene, was over there. The girl who had asked Jack the same question as the disappearing man. The question the frozen people had asked. And was the voice asking that question the same voice that had driven Mark Pickering into a bloody fury? The door Mark had tried to destroy with his face was the same door that had been pounded by invisible hands two nights ago. Who wanted to be let in? Or out?

Jack lowered his head and massaged his temples. The buzz at the back of his head had returned. Not a sound though. Something was on fast forward. A spool of unravelling thoughts, barely audible, almost intangible. Like reflections in a maze of dark mirrors.

"Jack, you okay?" Frank Blake asked.

Jack turned and looked at her. She was six inches shorter than him. Slim framed with a mop of untidy, thick dark hair. Her pale face with the dark eyes and the wide mouth, almost smiling, looked relaxed. As though yesterday had never happened.

"Ah, yes, yes," it took him a moment to focus and still the brewing storm inside. He shook his head. "How's Mark?" he asked.

"He's still over at the General," Frank answered. "He needed a little work done on that face. They kept him in. Two members of staff from our HDU are over there."

Jack rubbed his forehead where a dull ache was starting to throb. "Good, yea," he nodded. "No permanent damage then."

"Only what he did himself," Frank said. "Nothing you did."

Jack held her clear unwavering gaze for a moment but saw nothing there contrary to her words.

"Thank you," Frank said in a quieter tone. "The chance didn't arise yesterday."

Jack looked different to yesterday, Frank thought. He looked tired but something about his body language was wrong. His hands were restless, his eyes less steady than usual.

"You've been walking about quite a bit this morning," she commented.

Jack looked over his shoulder at the door briefly. "It's the ward," he said, "doing my head in today. Can't seem to find a quiet spot."

"Do you want to go for a walk, clear your head?" Frank suggested. "Off the ward I mean," she added. "Instead of pacing it." She looked around. "It's fairly quiet, we can get a little fresh air."

"I don't need an escort," Jack said.

"Maybe you need company," Frank answered.

Jack stood and watched as Frank exchanged words with her colleague in the office. Alison looked out at him once with a puzzled expression and then nodded at Frank.

Outside the ward Frank turned to walk down the corridor towards the main entrance of the hospital. The corridor was busy with people. Patients strolled along while a few members of staff hurried passed.

"Can we take a quieter route?" Jack asked. He indicated with his head the corridor behind them. It led to the rear corridor.

Frank shrugged her shoulders. "If you want," she said. "It doesn't go anywhere."

Jack turned and walked away. "What's the official verdict on what happened yesterday?" he asked.

Frank sighed and looked to her left. That side of the passageway was windows looking out onto an interior garden surrounded by the hospital buildings.

"Hysteria. Mass fainting," she told Jack. "Perhaps food poisoning."

"Food poisoning!" Jack sounded incredulous.

"I know!" Frank laughed.

"Four times now I've heard the same question asked," Jack said. He looked at Frank, gauging her response to this change of tack. Focusing on the problem seemed to still the brewing storm he had felt earlier inside him. The throbbing pulse in his head diminished.

"What question?" Frank asked as they rounded the corner into the back corridor.

"Do you know?" Jack said.

"Do you…" Frank began then froze, her eyes locked on something over Jack's shoulder.

"What's…?" Jack asked, turning to look down the corridor.

Standing with one hand on the door handle of the store room was the figure of an old man. He was very pale with a balding head. His suit, over a shirt and tie, looked old fashioned and dated. As Frank and Jack gazed at him he raised a hand to them slowly before opening the door and stepping inside.

## 25

"What is this?" Frank asked as Jack opened the door and stepped inside. Her heart gave a brief skip and a jump and she swallowed loudly. It crossed her mind that she had been lured here. She dismissed it. It was she who had suggested leaving the ward.

Jack stood in the open doorway. "Some sort of storage room," he said. "It was open once before when I passed. Old records and stuff."

"But that man?" Frank frowned.

"That I don't know," Jack answered.

Frank sniffed, noticing a change in the air.

"Pipe tobacco," Jack said nodding. He noticed the trace of anxiety lingering on Frank's face and wondered about it. Was it the smell or being alone here with him? Did she view him as a risk, like Pickering?

"I've smelt that before," Frank said and stepped around Jack into the room.

Inside it was gloomy and damp. Most of the space given over to boxes, some open topped, revealing piles of old clinical records and files. A long black torch was laid across the top of one of the boxes. Frank picked it up idly as she gazed around the room. There was no sign of the old man.

"Where did he go?" she asked.

Jack paced across the room and peered into the deeper gloom where it turned away in an L shape.

"No one here but us chickens," Jack said frowning.

Frank smiled. "My Dad used to say that," she told him. Her smile faded as she asked, "Was that the same man...?"

"The one I saw in the toilet block?" Jack nodded. "Pretty sure, yea."

Frank said nothing but her large eyes widened as she looked around.

"What is all this stuff?" She lifted a file from a box and flicked over the yellowing sheets. "It's ancient," she commented.

"I saw one about insulin therapy," Jack said.

Frank looked at him and shook her head. "That's pre-historic." She turned her attention back to the file in her hand. "Why hasn't all this been archived, shipped off?" she turned the pages of the file, frowning again.

"Cost probably," Jack said.

"What…?" Frank said distracted, her eyes scanning the file. "This is an ECT record," she paused as she read, "but it's a ward record. Odd. No individual patient records…Ah! I get it. That's not right."

"What?" Jack asked.

Frank dropped the file back in the bulging box. "It's a list of patients given ECT. A whole ward full almost. Indiscriminately."

"Shocking," Jack said and gave his lop-sided smile.

"It's not funny, Jack. It's like removing everyone's appendix because one patient has a stomach ache."

"Welcome to my side of the bed," Jack said.

Frank was about to reply when a sound from the corner drew both their attention. In unison they took a step backwards as the old man emerged from the shadowed corner of the room.

"Where'd you pop up from?" Jack asked.

Just outside the deeper shadows the man stopped and regarded them. Above the dark suit and tie his face seemed to glow unnaturally in the semi-darkness.

"Who are you?" Frank asked.

"I am the message," the man said in a voice that seemed out of sync with his lips.

Frank reached out a hand toward Jack as her heart began to thump violently. The room elongated, yet the face of the old man seemed to swoop forward. Clutching at her suddenly tightening and closing throat she tried to speak. She looked for Jack but he had disappeared.

Hands with grips of iron grabbed both of Frank's arms as others forced her head forward until she could only see the floor. The dirty, patterned, carpeted floor, as she was pushed rapidly forward.

"The Pad!" someone said.

"Hold her! Hold her!" A male voice said loudly and urgently. "I've the key."

Frank fought but those restraining her kept her head down and her arms painfully twisted into her back. A bunch of keys rattled and then a heavy door sounded, flung violently back on its hinges. She kicked out but other hands grasped her ankles. She was lifted and swung forward, the clamping hands on her limbs remained fixed.

"Pin her. Back hammers, please," the same male voice ordered.

Frank was pushed to the floor as her arms were further twisted and locked behind her. The weight on her legs shifted. A stray hand slipped in between her thighs and fingers probed upwards. Frank screamed and spat. The hands withdrew and a single body pressed her down. The weight on her legs, folded against her buttocks. Hands around the wrists of her locked arms. One, two, three. The weight pinning her bounced on her, squeezing the breath from her. Then suddenly withdrew. A door slammed and a key rattled in a lock.

Breathless and frantic Frank kicked herself onto her back. She was alone in a rectangular room. The floor and walls were a uniform dull red. Above a single bulb burned on the unreachable ceiling. The room was featureless. The door, merely

174

an outline on the wall, had no handle and a square window of almost opaque laminate with shutters outside.

Frank hurled herself at the Seclusion Room door and beat it with her fists. She screamed again. A sudden wave of fear and sadness swept over her and she sank to her knees, her eyes brimming with tears.

Something moved behind her and she looked over her shoulder.

In the far corner of the room a figure was standing. It was tall and shrouded in darkness. From beneath the heavy folds of a hood two points of dull light burned like blue fire. The thing extended a hand towards Frank and she screamed louder and more shrilly than ever.

"Frank! Frank!" Jack said loudly, gripping her by the arms and shaking her. "Are you OK?"

Looking dumbly around Frank found herself back in the corridor outside the closed door to the storeroom. She felt tired and pain arced across her shoulders and down her arms.

"What…the room?" She said.

"You had some kind of attack," Jack said, his face concerned. "A panic-attack. Hyperventilating." He let go of her arms as she slumped back, resting against the wall.

"The man. The old man." She took a shuddering breath.

"Vanished," Jack gave the closed door a glance, "a few seconds after he appeared."

Frank shook her head. She willed her breathing to steady. The pain receded from her arms. Her heart skipped then settled into a regular throb. What had just happened?

"We should get you back to the ward," Jack said.

Frank's eyes were deep, dark pools as she looked at him wordlessly.

"Do you have anxiety problems?" he asked.

Frank gave a weak smile. "Who's the bloody nurse here, Jack?"

They turned away from the room and began to move. Franks head was a swimming diorama of fractured images from her... dream... Vision?

"You think this is all anxiety?" she asked. "All in our heads?"

"I think something bloody peculiar is going on," he gave a harsh mirthless laugh as he parodied himself, "no one knows," he said.

"That question," Frank asked, reminded by Jack's remark, "Do you know?" Her heart was slowing and the images swirling in her mind drifting away like gossamer in a breeze. She shook her head.

"Yea."

"You said you'd been asked that four times."

Jack nodded as they reached the corner and turned back toward the ward. "The old man. The girl. Doctor Giles and the guys who had food poisoning," he accompanied the last with a sour smile.

"The girl?" Frank queried.

They reached the entrance to the ward and Jack pointed down the corridor with his thumb.

"That girl next door," he said.

"Emily," Frank said quietly as her fingers fumbled for the key on her belt.

26

For one of the few occasions in her professional life Frank went through the motions of her work with little thought to the twenty-plus men in her care. Her father's death and the breakdown of her marriage had had the same effect. She walked among the Harbour patients like a zombie, her mind elsewhere. As the late autumn afternoon outside the windows dimmed to dusk Frank was absorbed in events that had no basis in any logic or sense she could fathom.

Ghosts, dreams, hallucinations and the emergence of panic attacks. Was she on the wrong side of the bed, as Jack had said?

Frank ambled around the ward granting leave, answering queries and offering half-hearted reassurance to the men whose world was currently defined by the walls of the old hospital. She shrugged off her colleague's questions regarding her paler than ever face and tired look and went through the motions.

She stopped at the entrance to the dayroom and gazed in at the seated men. The muted TV was displaying one of the endless progression of daytime cookery or antique shows, Frank could hardly tell which. A dozen men, a range of ages and casual dress styles were scattered around the large room. Some stared blankly at the TV, a couple just stared blankly. Some were involved in quiet conversations. Sat apart in a high-backed chair, his back to the window, Jack raised his eyes from his lap and returned her gaze.

Jack wondered what Frank was thinking. How she was processing what had happened. For himself he knew one thing. In spite of the ticking over engine of his mind, his thoughts had resumed a restless churning on returning to the ward, he knew what ever was happening around him was not the product of a diagnosis. Things he had thought impossible were taking shape. He had lost Claire, but events implied that was only because she was somewhere he could not see.

"Frank!" Angela Simpson's voice rang down the corridor from her office.

Frank turned away from the dayroom and faced the ward clinical lead.

Angela was standing at the door to the office beckoning to Frank. She was a small slight figure with bleached, fair hair. As though reflecting her personality her body had a hard, angular look. Her thin face, with fine chiselled features, high cheekbones and a wide thin mouth, appeared stern. Her blue eyes challenging and direct.

Frank stepped passed her into the small office near the ward entrance.

"Just need a word, Frank," Angela said as she closed the door.

It was a small, cramped space. Desk, a few chairs, filing cabinet. The walls festooned with notices and leaflets. What wall space could be seen was the same drab, worn magnolia that pervaded the whole ward. Least welcoming in the confining space was the presence of John Lawless. The bulky hospital manager stood arms folded before the high, dirty window as he leant back against an ancient radiator.

"Take a seat, Frank," Angela said as she sat in her swivel chair in front of a computer monitor.

Frank looked at the smug expression on Lawless' face. "Do I need a union rep?" she asked.

Lawless made a snorting sound through his nostrils.

"Not at all," Angels replied. She tried a reassuring smile, but her thin mouth, red with lipstick, made only a knife slash approximation. "I need to ask you a few things. That's all."

Frank nodded.

"First," Angels held up a red nailed finger, "about yesterday."

"Ok."

Angela looked down gathering her thoughts.

"Mark Pickering alleges you stood by and let Trent assault him," Lawless said bluntly. He raised the eyebrows on his florid, double-chinned face.

"That's not what happened," Frank said over Angela's head.

"Jack did kick Mark, though, didn't he?" Angela asked.

"Dan had been knocked to the floor," Frank explained. "Mark was distressed and disturbed. He turned on me and I believe Jack just acted instinctively. Dan saw the whole thing."

"Steven's account," Lawless delivered this with a wan smile, "is a little hazy. To say the least."

"Jack acted…" Frank began but Angela interrupted.

"You took Jack off the ward earlier," she noted. "When some of the staff say he was looking agitated and preoccupied."

"He was over stimulated by the ward," Frank responded. "I thought he needed a break from it."

"Time to get your stories straight, you mean," Lawless commented.

"John!" Angela looked over her shoulder and spat his name.

Lawless shrugged his shoulders and shook his head.

"You're looking for problems when a bigger one is staring you in the face," Frank said.

"You came back to the ward looking flustered and agitated yourself, someone reported," Lawless said with mock concern. "Lover's tiff was it?"

Frank half rose from her seat. "You…"

"Alright!" Angela said loudly. "Enough." She turned in her chair to face the manager. "That's not helping, John," she said.

"Well," Lawless said, "as this doesn't seem to be getting us very far," his voice took on a sarcastic tone, "perhaps Staff Nurse Blake could tell us about a certain Gavin Darcy."

"Gavin…?" Frank asked.

"You do know him then?" Lawless' smile assumed another degree of smugness. "The local ghost buster who had to be asked to leave after attempting some half-arsed séance with Emily Greene. He seemed to be under the impression he had some kind of official sanction from you."

"Angela, he's twisting things," Frank said. A knot of anger was burning in her insides.

"Frank, you look tired," Angela said in a calmer tone. "I know night shifts don't agree with you. You're off tomorrow. I want you to go home and rest while I sort this out. I'm sure it'll all blow over."

"You're suspending me!?" Frank stood abruptly.

"I'll get to the bottom of this allegation and ring you at home," Angela announced with a degree of finality.

Frank walked to the door then turned back with one hand on the handle.

"This ship is sinking," she said, then looked Lawless in the face as she added, "I'm surprised you haven't been one of the first over the side."

In the staff changing room Frank wrenched open the door of her locker with sufficient force to make the row of battered, grey cabinets rock forward and thump back against the wall. Her eyes, in the small distorted surface of the mirror on the back of her locker door, seemed unnaturally large and bright with barely supressed tears of anger and frustration. She dragged her bag from the cabinet and slammed the door. She pulled her phone out as she strode into the corridor and saw that she had a missed call and two text messages from Gavin Darcy.

Both messages had arrived within two minutes of each other. Both read the same.

"Call me! Something is very wrong in that place."

More drama, Frank thought. More mystery. What she needed was someone to shine a light on things and make it all clear. The thought tripped a switch in Frank's head, reminding her of something.

## 27

Mick Draper's face, when it appeared in the six-inch gap between his front door and frame, was unshaven, red-eyed and looked older than the early forties Frank knew him to be. Recognising Frank he gave a grunt of surprise and pulled the door a little wider. When he opened his mouth to speak there was a waft of alcohol fumed breath. Cider, Frank decided.

Finding him hadn't been difficult. Asking a porter on her way out of the hospital had given her enough information. Tosh had known the road but not the house number.

"The old army Land Rover propped up on bricks on the front garden is as good as a signpost," he had laughed.

"What are you doing here?" Mick asked.

Frank paused as she marshalled her thoughts. She was certainly not going in if he was drunk.

"Who is it, Michael?" An elderly, female voice called from inside the house. It sounded hoarse and cracked, a testament to a lifetime of smoking.

"A nurse from the hospital," Mick said over his shoulder.

"Well, let her in," the woman called. "This dressing isn't going to change itself."

"Me Mam," Mick said and opened the door fully. "She thinks you're here to look at her leg ulcer." He shook his head. "They came this morning," he added. He was wearing jeans and a dark sweat shirt, sockless feet in grey slippers.

"Sorry," Frank said, "I shouldn't have bothered you."

"No, it's okay," Mick gave a slight smile, "I was a bit abrupt, sorry. Just surprised to see you here. Come in." He stepped back away from the doorway.

After a slight hesitation Frank stepped inside.

The door opened straight onto the living room. It was tidy with an old fashioned three-piece-suite in a floral design. The floor was carpeted in another, clashing, flower heavy pattern. There was a dark wood coffee table and a tall wall unit with a glass front. Every shelf had an arrangement of ornaments, most of which seemed to be elephants. In a high-backed chair, beside a muted TV, showing an episode of Murder She Wrote, an elderly woman was sitting. She had a halo of frizzy grey hair around a lined, sunken-eyed face. Her large purple cardigan covered a grey knitted top and hung down to the calves of her navy-blue trousers.

"I just wondered if you were ok," Frank explained. "No one had heard from you. And I think I came across your torch."

Mick looked at Frank's empty hands as if expecting to see the torch.

"Only cost me seven quid on E-Bay. I can live without it," he said.

"Where's your case?" The woman asked. "I can't afford to buy my own dressings." She glared at Frank and pointed at Mick. "And he's next to useless," she said.

Mick raised his eyebrows to Frank.

"You've had your leg done this morning, Mam," he said. "She's come to see me," he explained, "from St. Mark's."

The woman raised her face and emitted a breathless, cackling laugh. "Come to take you away, has she? I knew it would come to that." She smiled at Frank with stained, yellow teeth.

"Don't be daft!" Mick told his mother as he sat on the edge of the sofa. He indicated the chair to Frank and she lowered herself onto the front edge. His leg nudged a half-empty plastic bottle of cider standing beside the sofa and he picked it up and dropped it behind him giving a small, guilty smile.

"What happened, Mick?" Frank asked, then paused and gave the old woman a quick glance.

Mick gave his mother a look then said to Frank, "She's here half the time. Away with the fairies the other half." He gave his small smile again. "She was one of your lot," he explained. "Forty years at St. Mark's. Retired ten years."

Frank raised her eyebrows.

"She had me late on," Mick said. "My sister is fifteen years older than me. She used to work on the old elderly care villas. Mam, not me sister."

Frank nodded.

"I bet you can tell some tales," she said to the old woman.

"Lies?" the woman said. "Not me. Always a straight talker."

"See?" Mick shook his head.

Frank kept her eyes on the woman for a moment, hoping she wasn't seeing the future.

"Why did you walk out, Mick?" she asked.

"Why do you care?" Mick asked and rubbed a hand over his stubbled chin. "No one else does. Apart from worrying about covering my shifts. Not even a call from…" his voice died away and he looked down.

Frank felt a twinge of embarrassment. Maureen, she thought.

"I think I found your torch in a room on the back corridor…" Frank recognised the tone in her voice. She was fishing.

Mick opened his mouth but his mother spoke instead.

"That bloody place!" she said. "I've told him a hundred times not to dawdle down there of a night."

"Mam!" Mick shrugged his shoulders at Frank.

"The back corridor, Mrs. Draper?" Frank asked the mother.

"Joan," the woman said. "Mrs. Draper was my mother-in-law. The witch!" She laughed again.

"What's so special about that corridor, Joan?" Frank asked. She looked at Mick and he was sitting back, his eyes locked on his hands in his lap.

The old woman raised a hand and pointed at Mick. The joints of her finger were knotted and arthritic.

"I know why you came home in the middle of the night," she said. "You think I'm dementing." She smiled but there was no warmth in it. "You saw him. Just like I told you."

"Saw who?" Frank swung her eyes between the two.

"Miller!" Joan said.

"Miller?" Frank echoed.

"And you need to watch out too," the woman said to Frank. Her eyes had developed a new intensity and stared at Frank with a clear gaze.

"Who are you talking about?" Frank asked.

"Robert Miller," the woman answered. "Bob Miller. The old night supervisor." She waved a hand with a dismissive gesture. "Oh, gone, even before my time," she said, "but I heard enough about him. A martinet. Stomped about as if he owned the place. Pipe clenched in his teeth. Everyone danced to his tune. Patients. Staff. No one left, or did anything unless he said so." She took a ragged breath after this tirade and sat back in her chair. "Them days half the staff still called themselves Attendants," she said.

"What happened to him?" Frank asked.

"Died on the old villa. Dementia." Joan said. "But I know of people who've seen him since."

"Is that what scared you away?" Frank asked Mick.

Mick didn't answer. He looked at Frank blankly while his fingers toyed with the cap of the cider bottle.

"What did he look like?" Frank asked the woman.

Joan looked at Frank. It was an unpleasant gaze. A cat staring at a mouse.

"I don't think you need me to tell you. Do you?" she said.

Frank looked at Mick again but he was avoiding her gaze. She let her eyes roam around the room. The elephants, everything she noticed then, had a light coating of dust.

"Michael!" Joan said suddenly and loudly, startling Frank. "Get that stuff out of the unit. The old pictures."

Mick stood up hesitantly, giving Frank a fleeting, odd look.

"I didn't mean to upset anyone," Frank apologised. "I just…"

"Bottom cupboard!" Joan said, ignoring Frank. "The buff envelope. The big one."

Mick bent in front of the wall unit and from behind the sofa Frank heard him moving things around. He stood up with a large, dog-eared envelope in his hands.

"Hand it to her," Joan ordered her son. "What's your name again?" she asked.

"Frank… Frances."

"Let Frances see them photos," the woman told her son. "I was a ward sister," Joan said as Mick handed Frank the envelope. "When that meant something. Before the Nursing Process became Care Plans, and before we were managed by OTs and redundant supermarket managers. Before everything went to hell."

Frank spilled the contents of the envelope onto her lap as she looked at the old nurse.

"I got most of them when I retired," the old woman told Frank. "Took them from the Memory Cupboard." She gave a harsh, brittle laugh. "I knew the place would be knocked flat before long."

Frank shuffled the photographs, of various sizes, like a clumsy hand of cards.

"The one you're looking for is a group," the woman said. "Nurses standing in line. All in uniform. Half the group died in the Nurses Home fire."

Some of the photographs were of the hospital. Some of random people or ward interiors. The clothes and the décor generally dated, the pictures browned with age. There were two group shots. Assemblies of nurses standing outside hospital buildings, stiffly posing for the camera. Frank did not need to ask which one Joan wanted her to see.

In one photograph there was a figure she recognised.

At the extreme left of the front row of nurses a man was standing. He had a long, pale face beneath a domed bald head.

He stood firmly planted, legs apart and his hands grasping the lapels of his dark suit jacket.

"I never saw the old bastard," Joan said and emitted her dry, breathless laugh again. "I was never a one for overtime shifts."

Frank looked up from the photograph. Mick had retreated through a doorway at the rear of the room. Frank could see part of a kitchen. The cider bottle had gone with him. The old woman had lapsed into silence and gazed at Frank with eyes that suddenly seemed clouded and far away.

Tiredness overcame Frank, not unusual at this time of day after an early start, but the flutter of palpitations accompanying it made her anxious. She stood up, and babbled a thank you, sorry for intruding, farewell apology and let herself out of the house. As she passed the Land Rover in the garden, uselessly supported on bricks, she wondered who it made her think of more. The Drapers or herself.

As she fumbled in her bag for the car keys her heart began to speed up for no reason. The familiar tension returned to her throat and she swallowed loudly, with difficulty. She stood beside the car with one hand in her bag and closed her eyes.

Why was she here? What had she hoped to achieve? Confirmation that she had seen a ghost in the hospital? And had she? The panic attack, or whatever being enclosed in the storeroom had caused, had left her with only a memory of fear, claustrophobia and a feeling of helplessness. There had been an old man in the corridor, and the room. But could that really have been someone from a fifty-year-old photograph?

Frank slapped her palms on the roof of the car and leant against it. She took a breath and exhaled slowly, a long slow stream of air. Again. In, then out slowly. She counted in her head. Breathe in for five, out for ten. Get control, she thought. Of whatever Angela and Lawless had left her.

"Physician, heal thyself," she said with a sour smile.

28

The fact that Frank had disappeared half way through her shift did not go unnoticed by Jack. He wondered what had happened. She had come out of that store room looking shaken and confused. Some sort of panic attack, he guessed, after that old guy popped up again.

And what was that all about?

One minute the old man had been there and then, after Jack had turned to look at Frank, who was gasping for breath, he was gone. The more he thought about things the more puzzled and irritated it made him. And the more he became aware of that buzz in his head. The unwinding spool of control.

Standing at the entrance to the dayroom Jack let his eyes wander over the other patients. It was the same everyday scene. The hum of conversation. The rustle of newsprint. The electronic muttering of the TV. Outside, beyond the windows, the world remained uninspiring, uninviting. A grey, cold, pale watercolour of autumn.

When his name was called from the corridor Jack turned to face the ward sister, Angela, standing outside her office. He walked towards her after she raised a hand and beckoned him.

"Can I borrow you for a minute, Jack?" She came up to his shoulder. A thin woman who looked as though she had been chipped from a hard block.

"I have a few moments before my plane leaves for Bermuda," he said as he reached her.

Angela favoured him with a thin smile. Just an elongation of her blood red lips.

The office was a cramped space, needing redecorating and the walls de-cluttering. There was a faint whiff of body odour which Jack assumed was wafting from the figure of the hospital manager, Lawless, who stood, arms folded, leaning back against a radiator beneath the window. Angela, when she stood close to Jack to close the door, gave off an aroma that he thought was more Eau-de-Tart's- Handbag.

"You might want to move away from that radiator," Jack said, "smells like you're done."

Lawless snorted and said nothing.

"Take a seat, Jack," Angela indicated a chair as she sat at the desk.

"What's up?" Jack sat on the edge of the hard, wooden framed chair.

"What happened upstairs yesterday?" Lawless asked.

Angela cast him a quick glance, and a brief head shake, over her shoulder.

"Yesterday?" Jack replied with a blank expression.

"With Mark Pickering?" Lawless said.

"Oh," Jack nodded as if suddenly remembering. "When the six-foot outhouse decided to knock a door in with his face? When a snot-nosed kid and a young woman were left to deal with him because your alarm system failed and half the ward was pole-axed by food poisoning?"

"What did you do?" Lawless' eyes beneath the heavy lids stared at Jack.

"I helped the kid up so he could go get help," Jack answered. "When things calmed down a little."

"And Staff Nurse Blake?" Lawless queried.

Angela released a sigh and turned her chair a little. She gazed at the Trust Logo playing Pong on her computer screen.

"Does her job as well as anyone else on the staff," Jack replied. "Far as I can see."

"About what I expected," Lawless spoke to the back of Angela's head.

"How are you feeling this afternoon, Jack?" Angela asked, ignoring the manager. "You seemed a bit wired this morning."

Jack looked down at his hands. Involuntarily they had curled into fists. It wasn't the woman. Something about Lawless' attitude, his tone of voice, irked him.

"You know what, Ang?" Jack said and looked her in the eye. "I just lost my wife. I haven't seen my daughter for the best part of a month and I'm locked up with the cast of One Flew Over the Cuckoo's Nest. I think I'm entitled to be a bit 'wired'."

When the duo excused him, with the promise from Angela that she would speak to him later, Jack stopped a few paces away from the closed office door and looked back.

He had a pretty good idea what had happened to Frank. His intervention in the Pickering episode was obviously a problem. And it didn't take a great leap of the imagination to read in Lawless' attitude, and voice, a bug up his arse regarding Frank.

As he started back towards the dayroom Jack uttered a harsh, two-word expletive regarding John Lawless.

Fat was the least obscene of the words.

Their heads close together little Bernard and the thin, druggy guy, Tom sat in two of the few chairs in the room that had no direct line of sight to the TV. Jack paused momentarily in the entrance to the room then stalked across towards them. He was no longer in a mood for quite reflection. He wanted to shake the tree until answers began to fall.

"So, what's the view on yesterday's events?" He asked as he stood over the pair.

Bernard looked up with his familiar guilty expression. Tom kept his head down. His lank hair hung forward at the sides of his thin, pale face. Jack raised his eyebrows and gave a lop-sided smile.

"We were just talking about that," Bernard said.

"Really!?" Jack raised his hands, palms up. "And here's me thinking you were swapping recipes."

"We don't know," Bernard said. He looked bashful enough to make Jack rein himself in a little. "We can't remember much. Other than waking up tired and feeling weak."

Jack looked at the top of Tom's downcast head.

"You got any thoughts, Tom?" Jack asked.

The younger man looked up at Jack. His face was fixed, caught between a frown and a sarcastic smile.

"Nothing you're likely to believe," he said.

"You might be surprised," Jack said and sat down on Tom's free side.

"Tom thinks all of us who were," Bernard began then paused, trying to find the words he wanted, "well, you know, us who were effected, we're tired because they used us like batteries. Drained our energy."

"They?" Jack frowned.

"You know," Bernard repeated and looked up at the ceiling and pointed.

"I've researched this kind of thing." Tom said. He had dark eyes and his pupils looked too large to Jack.

"How, by ingesting home-grown medicines?" Jack asked.

Tom pulled down the corners of his mouth, shook his head and turned away.

"Mate," Jack said, wanting to bite his razor-sharp tongue, "ignore me. This place is doing my head in. I've seen my share of weirdness. Tell me."

"It's the building, Jack," Bernard chipped in, "the hospital."

"What do you mean?" Jack addressed his question to Tom.

Tom engaged Jack's eyes again, almost reluctantly.

"That door banging the other night," he said. "The weird feeling you get down the toilets."

"And that back corridor," Bernard added, returning to his favourite subject.

"But down here it's just noises and us lot acting weird," Tom continued as though Bernard had not spoken.

"And?" Jack wasn't following the drift.

"Look," Tom's voice took on an edge of frustration. "That door, where the banging was? Behind that, a staircase that's been there for yonks. The toilets. Never altered for years. The rest of the ward? Chopped up. Sub-divided. Altered, over and over." He looked at Jack as though what he was explaining was pure and simple logic. His face deadly serious. "They can't find their way around," he said. "Without getting into our heads."

"Ghosts," Jack said. "We're talking about ghosts in a mental hospital." There were two ways of interpreting that remark he realised.

"It gets better," Bernard said and rubbed his hands with what Jack thought was a theatrical touch. "Tell him about the woman," he said to Tom.

"What woman?" Jack asked.

Tom looked very hesitant and his eyes drifted away to the window. The hospital grounds beneath the grey sky. The stark, leafless trees.

"I haven't seen her," he said, his eyes still on the windows. "It's just a feeling. An impression. When," he looked at Jack then away again quickly, "when They are around."

"Who are you talking about?" Jack felt his heart rate increase slightly.

"I don't know!" Tom raised his voice and frowned. "A dark-haired woman. She doesn't belong with Them." He rubbed a hand over his pale, furrowed forehead. "She's not one of Them, but she's tied in somehow."

Jack offered no comment. He rubbed the back of his hand across his mouth. In the back of his head that loose wheel, the slipping gear, began to spin again with a grating buzz.

## 29

At 8pm that evening the wind was hurling rain against the windows of Frank's living room. With the blinds drawn, and the soft glow of the arched standard lamp illuminating the room, she sat looking at the muted TV with blank eyes as she sipped thoughtfully from a glass of red wine. It took the second chime of the doorbell to rouse her from her musing.

Frank opened the front door and stepped back as a gust of wind threw rain into the hall. Outside a figure in a long raincoat was half shielded by a large black umbrella.

"Frances," Joyce said as she raised the umbrella to reveal her face.

"Joyce," Frank said in surprise as she looked over the woman's shoulder inquiringly.

"It's just me," Joyce said. "Can I come in?"

"Yes, yes, of course," Frank stepped aside to allow the older woman across the threshold. "I'm sorry, Joyce," she apologised, "I was expecting someone else."

Joyce shook her umbrella out of the door before closing it. "Yes, I know," she said, "Gavin." She placed the large black handbag she was carrying on the floor while she removed her wet coat and Frank noted that her carefully styled, retro hair seemed untouched by the rain.

"How did you…?"

"Through the Church," Joyce explained. "The same one your Mum sometimes attends."

Frank nodded.

"Gavin rang me today when he couldn't get hold of you. And again, after you rang him, to let me know he found you. I thought it might be better if I spoke to you." She hung her coat over the post at the foot of the stairs and stood silently for a moment gazing upwards.

"Joyce?" Frank queried as the silence lengthened.

"Antique rose," Joyce replied.

"Sorry."

"Your walls," Joyce smiled. "They're the same shade I have in my hall.

"Oh," Frank laughed uncertainly. "Why are you here, Joyce?" she asked.

"Because I'm concerned and I don't think that Gavin fully understands the situation."

Frank indicated the living room, inviting her colleague inside.

"I was drinking wine. Would you like one?" Frank asked as they entered the room.

"Thank you," Joyce nodded and smiled again. "I think that might be a good idea."

In the kitchen Joyce leant against the worksurface as Frank poured wine.

"What is it you think Gavin doesn't understand?" Frank asked, handing over the glass of wine.

"Did you get into bother, inviting him onto the ward?" Joyce sidestepped Frank's question.

"No more than I already seem to have gotten myself into," Frank pulled a sour expression. She sat back on the sofa in the living room as Joyce settled in the large armchair across the room, her handbag perched beside her on the chair arm.

"And I didn't exactly invite him," she said. "I asked him for some advice."

Joyce looked down into her wine for a second. "It was bound to happen at some point, I suppose," she said. "He's very protective about Emily." She looked up at Frank and her eyes, in the pleasant, slightly masculine face, held a trace of something Frank found hard to identify. "He has an interesting theory about things," she told Frank. "About Emily and the hospital."

"You believe Emily is psychic," Frank said. It was not a question.

Joyce took a sip of wine and her eyes roved around the room briefly. "I think the world is a little more complicated than most people think," she said.

"And what does Gavin think?"

Joyce sat back in the deep chair and raised her already arched brows. She puffed out her cheeks then gave a weak smile.

"Gavin believes," she told Frank, "that the hospital is haunted. That the ghosts of patients passed are being disturbed by the move and the demolition work."

"Ghosts," Frank said quietly.

"Oh, Gavin doesn't use that word," Joyce said and waved a hand dismissively. "He talks about energy. Trapped energy. And how old buildings, stone and brick, can store it. Like a wall that has been in the hot sun all day."

"And how does Emily fit into this theory?" Frank had a sense that the slight disparaging tone in Joyce's voice was because she had another theory.

Joyce drank a little more wine and leant forward and placed her glass on the low table between them. "He has convinced himself, and Emily, that the voices she hears are the trapped patients. He says they want Emily's help to find peace. A new sanctuary."

"Asylum." Frank was not sure why that particular word had popped into her head at that moment.

Joyce gave a short, almost bitter laugh. "That's a word with more than one meaning," she said.

"You don't agree with him?" Frank asked.

"I think that it's dangerous to get too involved in these things," Joyce answered.

"In what way?"

"Emily believes this has something to do with Angels," Joyce rubbed her forehead as though explaining was a physical effort. "She mentioned that to you, and a cottage. She thinks they want her help."

"Yes," Frank nodded.

"And she thinks that help can only be given by people who are dead."

"Oh, God!" Frank looked at her glass and was a little surprised to see that she had drained it.

Joyce glanced up at the ceiling as though with X-ray vision she was seeing Georgie asleep upstairs. Her hand strayed to her large bag and the fingers tapped the scuffed leather.

"Now would be the time to step away from this, Frances," she said.

"If it involves a risk to a patient, you know I can't do that," Frank said.

The woman held Frank's eyes for a moment then nodded.

"It's possible to care too much, you know, Frances," she said.

"What do you mean?"

"Get too involved," Joyce explained. "Get to a point where you can't switch off. It can ruin your life."

"I know," Frank agreed. "But I have to do my job the best way I can. Sometimes you can't just stop being who you are because the shift has ended."

Joyce moved her bag from the chair and placed it in her lap.

"I should go," she said. "I just thought we should try and not involve Gavin too much." She smiled. "Things are complicated enough for Emily as it is. We are probably best placed to support her and help her get home. That's the important thing."

Frank nodded and stood up as Joyce did.

"I can agree with that," she said. Then she had to ask the question that had been on her mind since Joyce arrived. "Joyce, do you know about Bob Miller? He was an old supervisor…"

"I know who he was," Joyce acknowledged and smiled. "Don't pay attention to old hospital stories," she said. "The older staff have always liked to tease the younger with ghost stories.

The past can't harm anyone, Frances. It's the present and future we need to keep an eye on."

Frank nodded again as Joyce moved towards the hall.

"Give my love to your Mum," Joyce said as she shrugged her coat on. "I've taken enough of your evening up." She looked briefly up at the ceiling again. "Your time with the little man is precious."

After looking in on Georgie, snoring softly, and in sleep looking enough like his father to cause her a momentary pang of regret and pain, Frank stood at the side of her bed and gazed down at the folded back quilt and the soft, cream sheet. No dreams tonight, she wished herself. There was enough to process and worry about. Her discussion with Joyce had ended with them both anxious and unclear about what could be done to ensure Emily's safety.

Emily believed some supernatural entity was the threat. Frank had the burden of that possibility and the question of Emily's and her own sanity in even considering it. Not to mention the fact that she had been sent home with a flea in her ear.

With the Louisville Slugger again propped against her bedside cabinet Frank clicked off her light and lay looking up into the darkness. The profile of the grinning clown above her was little comfort.

When sleep descended like a cloak of invisibility Frank became someone else.

30

Elizabeth stood at the window of the dormitory and gazed out. On the grass, bathed in warm summer sunlight, a group of children were playing, supervised by a tall thin woman in a smart, stiffly starched uniform. The children were clearly laughing and calling to one another, but the sound was defeated by the glass. All Elizabeth heard was the cries of distressed women and the clattering rumble of a trolley across the hard floor of the ward.

One child in particular drew her eyes. A girl in a soft cream dress. Like the child Elizabeth had lost.

Closing her eyes, she tried to imagine that child. All that came to her were her dreams.

Often, she dreamt of the same woman. The strange young woman who walked with such confidence through the world of men. The woman who cared for her boy-child and tried to help those around her. A woman who, unlike Elizabeth, had purpose and strength, weary as she was with care and regret. Elizabeth woke from those dreams with a sense of fear and sadness. But sometimes with terrible, heart wrenching hope.

It had always been the same. Since they had cut her.

To still the screaming void, the anguish and pain. To stop her striking out and delivering her pain upon them they had dulled her and cut her. The silent, stealthy knives, sharp as needles and thin as paper had entered her head. What were they searching for? What had they stolen from her? Her soul. That was clear.

Had they not taken enough?

The pain of her separation from her new born girl-child had never been enough. Elizabeth knew her crime. She regretted it, but would never regret the result. Yet, they tortured her and revelled in her error. To give birth to a child beyond the bounds of matrimony was heinous to them. A sign of sin. The mark of a deranged and insanitary mind.

The punishment? A life in sanctuary. A place of refuge.

The Asylum.

Elizabeth's pain felt fresh and burningly new. It seemed only yesterday she had screamed and cried as her child was torn from her. Yet, as she pressed her hands to the glass before her they were aged, the joints swollen and arthritic, the paper-thin skin barely able to conceal the blue veins beneath.

Her only comfort was her Angel.

Elizabeth turned away from the window and looked at her bed. The thin, comfortless mattress and the hard metal head and foot.

He was not there.

Of course not. He never came to her now in daylight. It was only at night he appeared.

In the dark he stood beside her. His head bowed. A cowl covering his head. Shrouded in gloom as though he wore their shame. But his eyes regarded her with kindness and sorrow. His being gave her comfort. His noble face, scarred and careworn, gazed into hers as tears coursed from his eyes and fell to the cold linoleum floor.

Frank awoke without any gasp of fear or surprise. She emerged from her dream in silence and with a strange sense of calm. She felt only sadness and the tears streaming from her large, dark eyes.

Going through the minutia of her day, tending to Georgie, taking him to school, absently wandering around Tesco, Frank tried to grasp the disappearing, gossamer tendrils of her dream. They eluded her, but left a strange sense of understanding and calm she could not identify. Paradoxically

217

they also filled her with a mounting sense of dread and pending disaster.

Frank stood at the self-service check out in the supermarket and thought, I am finally losing it. Like I lost Dad and Peter. Am I finally losing my grip on reality?

Frank stood in the centre of her living room and looked down at the coffee table. Only one thing was different to how she had left it. The blinds were open, giving a view of the uncaring, bland frontages of the houses across the road. The haphazard cushions, a stark contrast to her Mum's artistically arranged soft furnishings, remained askew and erratically placed on the sofa and chair. Georgie's colouring book and a rainbow of felt tipped pens were scattered across the armchair. Only one thing was misplaced.

Frank found it strange, but not, surprisingly, unexpected. Even though she remembered placing it firmly on top of the toy box in Georgie's room.

On the coffee table a small red fire engine sat. The one that released a maniacal scream when the light bar on the top was pressed.

Frank dropped onto the sofa and closed her eyes. She was neither shocked nor confused when a voice interrupted the silence in the room. When she looked up her gaze was met by large, moist eyes in a pale lined face.

"You have work to do, Nurse," Bob Miller said.

31

Jack placed his cup of cold tea on the low squat table in front of him. He looked around the dayroom. Over a dozen men absorbed in the usual banality on the TV or chatting. Newspaper rustled. Cups and saucers chimed. Outside it was another grey day, everything looked dark and sodden from the previous night's heavy rain. The sky was a uniform grey and looked heavy as wrought metal.

Everything was normal.

Except that it was not.

Jack had woken to the still persisting hum of his thoughts as they churned over everything that had happened. When he moved he felt as though he were moving in slow motion. The harsh, metallic echo of his thoughts faster than his muscles responses. So, at first, he had not been able to decide whether it was himself or the ward that felt wrong.

It was the ward, he eventually registered.

Every now and then the background chatter would die away, or the picture on the TV would roll and dissolve momentarily. Some of the men cast odd looks over their shoulders at times, as if in response to hearing their names called. Young Tom, sitting apart in a corner of the room, stood periodically as though about to leave then sat back down, his lips moving silently. And something in the air felt different. Like a building static charge or the lull before thunder.

Jack turned his head at the sound of a slamming door out in the corridor. It was followed by a series of dull thuds. Overhead something fell heavily onto the floor in one of the dormitories. Every face in the dayroom turned to the ceiling.

"Come in," the meter man quipped, but without enthusiasm.

Jack jumped up from his seat quickly, half ducking, as a sharp crack sounded from behind him. The glass in the window had cracked diagonally from corner to corner.

Jack stepped into the corridor and glanced around for a member of staff. After a couple of paces he stopped and bent forward, hands clutching his head. He experienced the same attack he had after seeing Doctor Giles. He squeezed his eyes shut as a silent explosion detonated inside his head. Memories, images, snatches of conversations flew and bounced about in his mind like a scattered deck of cards. It was overwhelming. Every piece of information stored in his brain clamoured for attention. He heard voices calling and a loud, roaring masculine scream as he staggered sideways and fell against the wall.

Dropping to his hands and knees Jack opened his eyes, his vision clouded by tears. The floor was moving, rippling beneath his hands. Colour and texture alternated in jerking kaleidoscopic fashion. One second it was carpet, then tile, wood, linoleum, then back to carpet. He lifted his head from the confusion and looked forward.

The corridor was full of people. Bodies, some substantial and others like shadows, were moving randomly around the length of the passageway. As his eyes cleared, the torrent of images and sounds inside his skull diminished slightly. It became a background noise of voices and slamming doors. Somewhere crockery was rattling and something fell and shattered.

Jack tried to make sense of what he was looking at but his eyes delivered only confusion. The people in the corridor were not just moving about they were shifting images behind water, shattered glass, figures seen through a heat haze. Some were dressed, others in night clothes, a few in uniforms. Nurses and a couple of men in suits and stiff almost military dress.

A door opened in the wall beside Jack, where there was no door. An elderly woman stepped into the corridor. She leant close to him, her eyes wet and large, her mouth had only a handful of stained teeth.

"Where are we going?" she asked in a high, cracked voice. "Do you know?"

Jack reeled away from her and almost tripped over a man in tracksuit bottoms and a hoody crawling along the floor. Side stepping around the man Jack headed back to the dayroom.

"Where you going, can we come?" A different voice called at his back.

In the dayroom in place of the dark gas fire, in an open hearth, a fire was burning, stacked high with glowing coals. A man in a suit, the jacket adorned with short tails, turned and raised a hand in Jack's direction.

"Won't be a minute, old boy," the man called across the room, "just boiling the King's partridges."

Around the room people moved and sat. Jack had to concentrate to identify the patients he knew from the shifting, mutating images of the new additions. He stepped back as two men approached him pushing a trolley with a box the size of a coffin. The men wore thin, grey work coats. One taller than the other, with a drooping moustache, smiled at Jack as they passed.

"I only come for the tea and the milk," the moustached man told Jack.

Jack turned back to the door but it had gone. It was now a wall of heavily patterned wallpaper on which a round wall light glowed softly. A small thin man in a uniform like a zoo keeper pointed up at the light.

"It's the moon," he said. "Never have a quiet night when it's full."

Jack turned again and the open fire had gone. The cold gas fire had returned, surrounded by a high mantlepiece on an ornate, white fire place that was not there. Along the shelf above the fire a large ginger cat wove sinuously between ornaments and a pair of china vases.

"Molly's upstairs in the coal shed," a woman shouted and began to laugh in a high-pitched cackle. She pulled the moth-eaten fur coat she was wearing tight to her body as she ran across the dayroom. She vanished into the wall beside the chimney breast.

Jack covered his eyes and tried to still his mind. He felt a wave of nausea as on a bucking boat. The sounds continued. Voices. Doors. The rattle of trolleys and footsteps on hard wooden floors. From above came the sound of glass breaking.

"What the hell…" Jack said through gritted teeth.

A hand fell on his shoulder. "LSD," the meter man said, "they've spiked the tea. I knew they were doing it all along." He turned and walked into the corridor, through the arch that was no longer a wall.

Jack followed him but he had vanished among the throng in the thoroughfare. Where was he? Where…?

Jack suddenly felt that he was slipping, losing his grip on something. A terrible abyss awaited him beneath a cliff on which he was scrabbling for purchase. A desperate need to cling on swamped him. Safety, reality was being dragged from his grasp as he slithered towards a fearful precipice. He had to find the way to safety. But where was that?

No one knew.

Another hand landed lightly on his arm and Jack felt a sudden wave of grief sweep over him. It was Claire.

"Concentrate, Jack," she said, "you have to help her."

32

Frank stopped her car outside the entrance to the hospital blocking the exit of two other vehicles. She sat for a moment behind the wheel and gazed at the dull, yellow glow of light inside the glass porch. She did not know why she was here. The cryptic message the old man had delivered before disappearing as she blinked could have meant anything. Yet Frank knew she was in the right place at the right time. It was the certainty of a delusion she thought as she climbed out of the Volkswagen.

Frank pulled her phone from the pocket of her coat as it emitted a bleeping cry for attention. The text message from her Mum, confirming that she would collect Georgie from school, was concluded with a question mark and three exclamation marks.

"If you're going down to the ward," the woman behind the reception desk called, recognising Frank as she passed, "ask them to answer the phone. Five calls I've tried to transfer and no one is picking up."

When she reached the T junction and turned towards the ward Frank could see that something was happening further down the corridor. Outside the entrance to the female half of the Harbour four women were standing. One was crying while another tried to comfort her, an arm across her shoulders. The women watched Frank pass with wide eyes, saying nothing.

On the floor, close to the male entrance, a man in tracksuit bottoms and a hooded top was crawling along the floor. Another patient standing with his back to the wall of windows on the left, dank shrubbery and the threatening sky behind him, watched Frank approach.

"Don't go in there, Nurse," the man said and pointed at the ward door.

Frank slowed and looked at the two men. She was about to bend to the crawling patient when the ward door began to slam repeatedly.

"Why is that door not locked?" Frank asked.

Neither of the men responded.

The door stopped banging and remained closed as Frank stepped up to it. The thin, vertical window on the handle side was broken, the glass starred and lined. It obscured her vision as she looked into the ward. For a moment the corridor beyond seemed full of moving bodies. Refocusing Frank saw a few people wandering the corridor, their images fractured and blurred by the thick shattered glass. The door moved freely when she pushed it and she walked into the ward.

Behind the door Ben Shelton was standing with his back to Frank as he ran one hand over the blank wall before him. In his other hand he held his door key.

"Ben," Frank touched the young man's arm and got no response. "Ben! What's going on?"

The nursing assistant looked at her without recognition and turned back to the wall. His fingers crawled across the surface as he pushed the key against the wall.

"I can't open the door," Ben said. "The key won't go into the lock. We have to get out."

Frank looked down the corridor. There were a couple of white plastic alarm fobs laying on the floor. They had been pulled, but no alarms were sounding. Two other men were moving along opposite walls, feeling there way with searching fingers like blind men. In the centre of the passageway an older man turned in circles as he pointed to the ceiling. Frank recognised them all but none responded to their own names as she began to move among them.

The clinic door, on Frank's left, was standing open. Inside Alison Pink was standing staring straight at Frank as she held an empty plastic jug.

"Alison!" Frank called.

The fair-haired woman smiled. "Take the medication, Frank," she said. "Take it or they'll never let you out again." The stare of her eyes seemed unfocused and the smile a rictus grin.

Frank backed away and moved to the next door. Angela's office. It was locked. Looking through the narrow window Frank saw John Lawless. He was standing in the corner of the room, squeezed between the end of the desk and the wall. He stared at Frank, unmoving.

"John, what is happening?" Frank called through the window as she pulled her key from her waist and inserted it in the lock. Inside Lawless raised his hand and made a shooing gesture. Frank's key refused to engage fully into the lock. It would not turn. There was a key in the inside she realised.

From the direction of the dayroom a voice called out. It was a woman's voice, followed by a peal of cackling laughter. Were there visitors on the ward too? Frank wondered. She headed towards the sound.

"Drugs, that's what it is." Bill Marsh, the wards resident joker emerged from the dayroom and came towards Frank. "Giles is experimenting on us all." He pushed passed Frank, headed to the exit.

Something fell heavily above Frank's head in the dormitory and there was the sound of breaking glass. She looked up and almost collided with Jack as he came from the dayroom. His face was ashen and he stared at Frank with no sign of knowing who she was.

"Concentrate, Jack," Frank said touching his arm, "you have to help me."

He looked at her and his eyes seemed close to tears. "Claire," he said.

"It's me, Jack, Frank!" she shook his arm. "We need to get help."

Jack rubbed a hand across his face. His eyes wandered over Frank's shoulder to the corridor beyond. Finally, he focused his gaze on her as she continued to pull at his arm. Wobbling he reached out and steadied himself with a hand against the wall.

"Do you see them?" he asked. "The ward's full of…"

231

"It's just the other patients, Jack." Frank looked quickly around them. "But something is wrong."

"Ah!" Jack slapped his palm against his forehead. "I heard Claire's voice. I saw her."

"She's not here, Jack." Frank turned his head, making him look her in the eye. "She can't be here. You know that. She's…"

The confusion in Jack's eyes cleared as the familiar spark of anger flared briefly in place of it. "You think I don't know that!" he said loudly.

"Come with me!" Frank clamped her hand around Jack's wrist and pulled him away from the dayroom. She led him down towards the staff office as she pulled her key free of the fob again.

"Where are we going?" Jack stumbled slightly as he matched her hurrying steps. His voice was that of someone emerging from sleep.

"You're ringing for the police and ambulance," Frank said as she unlocked the door and pushed it aside with her shoulder. "That phone on the desk." She pointed across the untidy office. "Four nines," she explained hurriedly, "you need an outside line." She pushed Jack across the room.

"Where are you going?" Jack looked at her, one hand lifting the receiver.

Frank stood in the open door of the office and turned her head to look down the corridor at the connecting door.

"Emily," she said.

## 33

"I have no bloody idea," Jack said angrily into the phone. "Food poisoning. A gas-leak." He paused for a moment listening to the questioning voice at the other end of the line. "Yes," he said with a sardonic smile, "that's correct. My name is Giles, Doctor Cornelius Giles."

After thanking the emergency services operator Jack put down the phone and walked to the open door of the office. He felt tired and his legs were shaking slightly. Propping himself up, his hands on each side of the door frame, he looked up the corridor. Men were still wandering around in the dayroom, a few standing transfixed gazing at things he could no longer see. The young guy, Tom, was standing in the centre of the dayroom one arm raised above his head.

Jack uttered a short, crude curse and walked back and flopped into the swivel chair at the desk.

He had seen Claire. He had heard her voice. Before she had morphed, like some cheap CGI effect, into Frank. Then his anger had overwhelmed his grief. The loss of Claire swamped by his rage at Fate, God…whoever it was that had torn her from his life. He sat back in the chair and took a long breath. His anger still lingered, and it quelled the buzz and the uneasy rise and fall of his thoughts.

"She's gone!" Frank stood in the doorway and looked at Jack with a wide-eyed anxious expression.

"What do you mean?" Jack asked.

"It's the same next door," Frank told him. "Everyone is in some sort of trance. A fugue state. No one's making any sense. I went all over the ward. Emily is not there."

"If she has any sense she'll have gone home," Jack said.

"I don't think so," Frank replied. "I think she wants to kill herself."

"She could be anywhere," Jack said.

"Oh, God," Frank said and raised her hands to her mouth. "Where though?"

Frank's anxiety was tangible and stirred Jack's memory. His conversation with Wendy. "She went the wrong way…" he said.

"What?"

"The store room on the back corridor," he said.

At the exit from the ward Frank stopped. She looked back at the confused, wandering men she was leaving. "Damn it!" she turned anxious eyes on Jack. "I can't just leave. They need help. The alarms haven't worked, but we need to find Emily."

Jack rubbed a hand over his mouth as his eyes moved from side to side. He stepped back into the ward. On the wall was a small red box. On a rectangular window on the front was written; In Emergency Break Glass. Swinging his elbow Jack smashed the glass. Immediately the air was filled with the loud clamour of the bells of the fire alarm.

"Oops!" Just for a moment the familiar, twisted smile flickered across Jack's face. "Always shout fire in an emergency," he said, "it gets everyone's attention."

They ran, Jack on legs that did not feel up to the exertion, along the carpeted corridor until they reached the cold vinyl floor of the rear corridor. The insistent ringing of the fire bells echoed around the cold, hard walls. As they swung around the bend Jack stumbled and slid, crashing against the wall before righting himself. He came level with Frank as she stopped outside the open door of the store room.

"Emily?" Frank called and approached the dark opening.

Jack took a moment, bent forward, hands on his thighs, to catch his breath, then he followed Frank through the doorway.

The room was empty. The gloom inside, the cold damp air, just as when they were last there. Some of the boxes had been tipped over. The floor was more littered by files, spools of tape and loose sheets of paper. Mick Draper's long black torch was on the floor among a mass of unwound tape. Jack walked passed Frank and looked into the dark corner of the room. There was no one, nothing, there.

"Where is she?" Frank asked.

Jack walked back out into the corridor and swung his head in both directions.

"This is hopeless." Frank stepped up beside him.

"What makes you so sure she is going to harm herself?" Jack asked.

Frank looked down at the floor and shook her head. She wasn't sure where to begin.

Jack crossed the corridor and stood at a window. He rested his hands on the sill, supporting his weight, his flagging strength. The ward had drained him, he thought.

"Frank." His voice was quiet but had a note of urgency.

Frank looked at Jack, his eyes fastened on the window, and stepped towards him.

Outside was the fenced compound containing staff cars. In the middle of the carpark Emily was turning around slowly as though lost, or searching for something. Frank watched her then looked passed her. Behind the cars was a high, metal mesh fence. Outside that there were a few large trucks parked, the vehicles belonging to the demolition team. Beyond that there was the steep, darkly tiled roof of a small building. It was the disused, long abandoned, mortuary.

"Rose Cottage," Frank said.

"What?" Jack gave her a puzzled look.

Frank, still with a trace of anxiety on her face, smiled thinly. "It's the name the staff used to refer to the mortuary. Rose Cottage."

"Emily!" Frank called across the carpark as she and Jack spilled out of the back door of the hospital.

Emily spun to face them. Her long, dark hair whipped across her pale face. Her eyes were huge and looked confused. She looked small and vulnerable, her thin body, in T shirt and jeans, visible shaking.

"I have to go to the Angel," she said.

"No." Frank's voice was firm with no trace of the anxiety her face betrayed. "Not on your own."

"I can help them." Emily lifted her hands and crossed them over her heart. "End this," she said.

Frank walked up to the girl and took hold of her hand. She looked towards the mortuary. "Together," she said.

Jack stood behind the two women as they stopped outside the door of the building. The wood was covered with peeling blue paint. The external hinges were red and flaked with rust. A large hasp and padlock secured the arched door. The stonework around it was dark and damp, moss grew along the edges of the blocks framing the doorway. The building looked like a small church with thin, arched windows and a steeply pitched angular roof.

"He's inside," Emily said.

"In a morgue?" Jack queried.

"It hasn't been used for years," Frank said. "It was a sandwich shop for the staff for a while," she added and smiled thinly at her own inanity.

"Let's hope they were using fresh meat," Jack said. He stepped forward and aimed his foot at the pitted, discoloured lock.

34

Jack pushed the door open. It hung awkwardly on the rusted hinges and grated across the floor. It stopped after half a metre and created a dark aperture into the building.

Frank looked at Emily and saw her own anxiety reflected in the girl's face.

"We have to," Emily said. Behind her a truck passed, its rear pilled with rubble.

"In for a penny…" Jack said with a strained smile.

Frank stepped through the opening and entered the mortuary.

The floor of the empty space was littered with debris. Bricks, pieces of wood and shattered plaster were strewn around. Patches of the walls showed exposed brickwork where the surface had crumbled and fallen. An ancient metal trolley, long enough to accommodate a body, lay on its side near the centre of the room. To one side a pile of plasterboard panels, large enough to have been a dividing wall, were stacked, leaning on the mildewed wall. The size and shape of a small chapel, the building was dark as twilight. The only illumination coming from bars of dull daylight entering through gaps in the boarded windows and from the half open door.

Emily walked passed Frank and stood in the centre of the empty space. After a failed attempt to widen the gap between door and warped frame Jack took a few steps into the mortuary.

"Why this place?" Frank asked. Her voice echoed around the bare walls. "There's nothing here."

"It's old." Emily turned her pale face and the large eyes on Frank. "Just the original walls and the roof."

"Look up there." Jack pointed to the exposed wooden beams of the steep roof.

Against the damp marked planks of the roof, between the support beams, were clusters of small dark shapes, suspended like rotten fruit.

"Bats!" Emily announced.

"Yea," Jack gave a tight smile. "Very appropriate."

Frank approached Emily and took hold of one of the girl's hands.

"Why did you need to come here, Emily?" she asked.

"The Angels…" Emily answered hesitantly.

"There are no…" Frank began.

"Frank." Jack's voice was low but held a note of alarm.

When Frank looked at him he was scanning the walls, his eyes following his moving, extended finger. She felt Emily's grip tighten around her hand.

The walls were moving.

All around the building, at irregular intervals, the walls were bulging. Pushing inward as something began to come forward into the mortuary. Slowly the eruptions took shape as they emerged from the cracked and dirty plaster. The shape they assumed was human, like crudely formed, life size, featureless, clay figures. Three dimensional shadows. Although they had no eyes the shape of the heads was sufficiently formed that the movement, as they all faced Frank and Emily, was discernible.

"We need to leave now!" Jack said from behind Frank.

Frank felt the now familiar kick start of her heart and the tightening of her throat and chest. She took a ragged breath. Backing away from the figures she pulled Emily with her.

"They're behind us as well," Emily said. "Everywhere!"

In unison the figures took a staggering, almost reluctant, step away from the walls and moved closer.

"We're getting you out of here." Frank tried her best take-your-medication voice, but there was a tremor in it.

"It's not her they want, Frances." Joyce pushed the door closed with her back as she spoke.

She looked just as when Frank had last seen her. The raincoat over dark trousers and top. Her hair styled and sprayed into a stiff helmet around her head. The same heavy black bag clutched before her. For a moment she just stood and looked at them all.

"You've done what was needed, Emily," Joyce said with a soft smile. "Thank you."

"Joyce, what's going on?" Frank's anxiety was building, and a tiny spark of anger.

"Would you have come here if I'd suggested a walk to an abandoned mortuary?" Joyce asked.

"Ok, enough!" Jack took a step towards Joyce. The anger in his voice was clear. "We are out of here. Move aside, Dame Edna!"

"You have no leave, young man!" Frank did not really need to turn to identify the source of this new, loud voice. It had arrived accompanied by the strong, unmistakeable aroma of burning tobacco.

Bob Miller was standing in place among what was now a circle of grey sentries surrounding Frank, Jack and Emily. His eyes, in the long, thin, pale face were burning with intensity. He stood, firmly planted, legs slightly apart, his hands gripping the lapels of his ancient suit jacket.

Jack was about to utter an appropriately barbed comment when he was assaulted again by that wave of sensation, emotion, memory and images. More intense than ever it struck him like a physical blow and he bent forward clutching his head. The persistent ticking over of his mind, stilled in the last few minutes by activity and purpose, swelled and swamped his will and control. He grunted and collapsed to his knees.

Frank took a step towards Jack and stopped as she felt Emily release her grip and move away from her. The girl was approaching the nearest grey figure with shuffling steps, the gait of a sleepwalker.

Frank felt her anxiety spike as she swung her head trying to understand what was happening. Jack on his knees, head in hands. The old man standing gazing down at him. Emily reaching a hand towards the strange grey shape before her. Joyce, an odd, sad smile on her face, advancing across the dusty floor.

"All the wrongs done in this place," Joyce said as she stepped into a space in the circle of figures, "for the right reasons." She reached up and gently touched the face of the nearest grey, shadowy figure. She smiled briefly as if recognising a friend. "Mr. Miller has tried to show you, Frances," she said. "All the brutal, crude efforts made, over the years to care for and cure the patients." She looked briefly over her shoulder, at the door, or the hospital beyond the walls. "And now, on the eve of All Saints Day, how do they repay that debt?" She smiled at Frank, but it did not touch her eyes. "They revolt in panic. Swarming over the hospital like maddened wasps, seeking escape, because the nest is being destroyed." Gently she stroked the arm of the figure beside her. "As though they would ever desert them."

"Who are they?" Frank pointed at the grey shape beside Joyce, feeling her knees tremble, strength drain from her body.

"Your colleagues," Joyce said, her hands moved restlessly over the large bag in her grasp. "Emily's Angels. Nurses who died with regret in their heart, unfinished care or the guilt of neglect. Marshalled by Mr. Miller to finish their business. To fulfil their duty of care. For eternity."

Frank felt a momentary lapse in her fear. Joyce's manipulation of her fuelled the spark of anger that lay beneath her confusion and anxiety.

"So why bring me here?" She asked firmly. "And Emily and Jack?"

"Emily was a guiding light. She brought you here. Jack…" the woman looked down at the curled figure as he trembled on the floor, "Jack has a purpose in all this. He will be the reason you joined Mr. Miller's legion. As far as the world is concerned." Joyce released the clasp fastening her large black bag. "Someone needs to guide the patients, Frances. Bolster the ranks and lead everyone to the new hospital and the future. He can release you from the fear He has sown inside you."

247

Frank took a step away from Joyce. A swift glance showed her Emily like a statue, hand to the face of a clay-like figure, Jack a trembling child, Miller glaring down with open malevolence.

"New blood, Frances," Joyce said, "that's what's needed." The knife she drew from her handbag had a blade long enough to catch even the subdued light within the mortuary.

## 35

Through the chaos engulfing his mind Jack could hear voices. He dug his nails into the hard, rough surface of the mortuary floor and tried to focus, overcome the whirlwind trying to sweep him away.

"Why would you do this?" Frank asked.

"Brian is dying," the older woman replied. "He's afraid. They'll care for him. Make sure he finds peace, and not join the wandering, lost souls your mother seeks comfort from."

"Let Emily and Jack go," Frank said.

"They can't leave, Frances," the woman said. "No more than you can. You're perfect. Your Dad is waiting for you. Your life is in tatters. Failed as a wife. Suspended. Sylvia spends more time with your son than you do." She raised the pointed blade of the knife and fastened her eyes on the tip. "No one would be surprised if you did it yourself. That might spare Jack and Emily. Then you could do the only thing you know how."

"The girl is lost to us now," a male voice said. "John Trent will wake with no knowledge, his bloodied hand clasped around a knife. His life was always forfeit."

"And my son?" Frank asked. Jack could hear, even over his own tumbling thoughts, the tremor in her voice.

"I'll make sure Sylvia copes with that," Joyce said.

"You're mad!" The venom in Frank's voice was a testament to her anger.

Anger that kindled a flame inside Jack. Recognising it, remembering it, the fuel that focused him, overrode the chaos. He pushed himself away from the floor and straightened his arms. They were going to have him blamed for murdering Frank. And the girl, probably. One more headline about a deranged mental patient who had killed. As though it weighed one thousand pounds Jack raised his head on his straining neck. He saw Frank and Joyce, face to face, the older woman holding a long, wicked looking knife before her. But it wasn't that that drew his eyes. It was the girl. Emily.

Emily dropped her hand from the face of the featureless creature beside her. She looked at Jack and the dark, bottomless pits of her eyes saw into him. Through him. She smiled softly as her lips moved soundlessly.

"They don't want this." The voice that entered Jack's head, bypassing his ears, was Claire's. "They're tied together. Not by love, like you and me, but by duty and fear. Free them and save them. Concentrate. Help her."

Jack pushed himself to his feet. He looked at the figure of the old man, glaring at him. The image stepped away from him and shimmered, as if viewed through a heat haze. The storm inside his head abated as his eyes fastened on the cold, hard reality of the pointed steel of the knife.

Frank stumbled back away from Joyce. The threat of being torn from George's life fuelled a fire that almost swamped her fear. Yet, in spite of her anger at the injustice of the situation her legs betrayed her and she tripped, falling backwards. The older woman's eyes stared at her, blankly, uncaring, like an attacking shark. The knife descended, the blade sharp enough to slice the atoms in the air.

Jack's hand fastened around Joyce's wrist and halted the thrusting blade as his other hand, balled into a fist, swung at the woman's face. Still weak, his mind desperately refocusing, he over balanced and toppled against her. Joyce screamed as their bodies contacted and fell, the razor-sharp blade of the knife clasped between them.

"Jack!" Frank lurched to her feet and took a staggering step towards the fallen bodies.

Jack rolled onto his back and looked up at Frank. His face was ashen and his smile a mirthless grin. He threw the knife away from him, it hit the floor and skipped across the chamber with a sharp clattering sound.

"Every time you need help I end up in a fight," he said.

The air inside the building seemed suddenly turbulent. There was a sound like a gently hurrying breeze. Or a huge collective sigh. It was followed by dragging, halting footsteps as Emily crossed the room, almost staggering, and sat down heavily on the side of the overturned trolley.

The circle of shadow figures broke apart and the they began to move towards the wavering image of Miller. Two or three, as they passed Emily, reached out a faint suggestion of a hand which made the girl's hair lift and stir in a gentle breeze. Miller turned his stare on Frank until he was hidden by the clustered shadows around him.

The mass of shadow became a nebulous cloud which faded slowly as it sank to the ground and vanished.

"No, no, no..." Joyce's voice was more moan than articulated words. She pulled herself on to her hands and knees as she surveyed the chamber. Tears welled up in her eyes. "You promised!" she wailed.

"They're gone!" Frank got to her feet as she scanned the mortuary. Her fear had been swept aside, though her hands trembled with the excess of adrenaline in her system. There were only the four of them in the building. The amorphous, shadowy shapes, Miller, had all disappeared.

"They're free." Emily sat with her head down, her hands hung limply between her legs. Her voice came from behind the curtain of dark hair hiding her face. "Shades of care," she said, "things trapped here and controlled by the old man. Caught in his own need to hold onto the patients. To retain a purpose." She took a long, slow breath. "They're all gone now."

Joyce gave a high-pitched cry and curled up on the floor. Her voice had a dreadful sound to it. It was loss. The loss of hope.

Jack felt an odd calm descend on him. An unfamiliar silence inside his head. As though a storm had passed. I'm not mad, he thought, but the world is. He had felt Claire's presence again, had felt that purpose inside him she inspired that was not defined by his diagnosis. That free-spinning wheel in his head might always be there, but it wasn't who he was. It was just a small part of what he was. He watched Frank approach the seated girl and when she stumbled slightly he steadied her with a hand on her arm. She smiled at him briefly.

"What did you do," Frank asked Emily, "how do you know they are gone?"

Emily raised her head and the dark hair parted revealing a face that was paler than ever, the eyes larger and darker, and the expression serious, looking much older than her nineteen years.

"I made them a promise," she said.

Emergency services yesterday rushed to attend a major incident at St. Mark's hospital. The fire service and three emergency ambulances were mobilised to deal with events that resulted in a number of casualties and the closure of the access road to the hospital.

A spokesperson for the fire service stated that it appeared that demolition work at the site, originally the Victorian County Asylum, may have exposed underground pipe work and released a noxious substance. The gas released is believed to be responsible for the eventual collapse and bizarre behaviour of a number of staff and inpatients of the hospital.

No fatalities are reported but some staff and patients remain in the nearby general hospital under observation. One female staff member remains unconscious, but stable in intensive care.

An eye witness to the events, for confidentiality reasons named only as Jack, stated that the incident had been mismanaged by the hospital administration and blamed the near catastrophe firmly at the feet of the current hospital manager, John Lawless.

A spokesperson for the NHS Trust advised that they were aware of shortcomings in the present managerial structure of the hospital and were taking steps to address this issue. They went on to add that emergency procedures within the hospital had been effective and prevented any fatalities or permanent damage from the incident.

The 110-year-old building is now scheduled for demolition, the patients to be relocated to a new multi-million-pound facility 500 metres south of the existing site.

YESTERDAY.

Frank pushed the file on her desk away from her and reached across and straightened the picture of Georgie in his school uniform. She sighed. The sheets of printed paper in front of her drew her eyes back to them. She spun the pen held in her fingers back and forth then clamped her teeth around the already bitten cap.

The Serious Untoward Incident investigation into Liam Carson's death was pretty much concluded. The recommendations Frank and the SUI team would append to the document had yet to face the scrutiny of the Coroner's Court, but she doubted that there would be any great changes to be made.

It was a sad fact of life. Liam had taken his own life, while on leave from hospital, in response to psychotic delusions. No one could have adequately predicted or prevented the tragic outcome.

Frank picked up the file from her desk, carried it across the room and locked it in her filing cabinet. Apart from the glow over her desk from the lamp the office was almost dark. Outside the first-floor window the late afternoon January sky was a mass of high cloud, dark above and a sickly yellow illumination below. Beneath the window the hospital plaza and carpark were dusted with a fine coating of frozen snow.

Frank turned off her desk lamp and locked the office door behind her. The corridor was still fully lit but she was about the only person still on the floor. The lights would remain on until the last of the housekeeping staff had finished for the night. The sound of her heels echoed around the building as she walked to the stairs and down to the ground floor.

In the wide, high-ceilinged main corridor on the lower floor Frank took a glance at her watch as she moved towards the exit. She was running a little late but had wanted to be fully up to speed before she attended the meeting with Liam's family and the Advocacy Service. The meeting had been scheduled for five-thirty because both of Liam's parents worked full time.

Frank smiled to herself as she remembered her telephone conversation with George earlier. His response to her query about what his Gran was making for his tea had amused her.

"It's the famous pink sausages in cardboard, Mum," he had said, "we'll save you some."

When the electronic lock, on the door into the hospital main reception, clicked open in response to her ID card Frank turned and looked back down the long corridor behind her. She thought she had heard something. A soft rustling like the movement of cloth over the vinyl floor. The corridor was empty and the winter wind whispered passed outside. Just the wind, she thought. A blast from the past.

Frank crossed the reception area. It was deserted at this time of day but for the solitary security man behind the chest high desk, the office behind him pooled in shadow. Ahead of her was the shuttered entrance to the café. To her right a wide passageway led down toward the wards. It was bright and artfully decorated with enormous prints of photographic work by a prominent, and expensive, local landscape photographer. Just passed this turning was the entrance to the office of the recently revamped advocacy service.

Frank gave the new logo a quick glance as she pushed the door open. The re-design reflected the change the old voluntary service had undergone as new blood was recruited, adding a new dynamic to what had become a staid and plodding organisation.

Inside the space was like any other office anywhere in the world. Desks, computers, walls decorated with notice boars, white boards and leaflets advertising everything from psychotherapy to foot massages.

What was different this evening was that one desk had been pushed aside to accommodate a row of half a dozen extra seats. The metal framed, plastic chairs occupied by the parents and two sets of Aunts and Uncles of Liam Carson. The six relatives turned their heads in unison as Frank entered, then refocused on the young woman sat before them.

Frank smiled and muttered a brief apology for her lateness. She looked across the room and gave a nod of her head. On the opposite side of the room, leaning back against the wall, Jack winked at Frank and raised a finger to his eyebrow before offering her a brief salute.

"This hospital," a woman with a head of carefully styled grey hair picked up a tirade that had clearly been interrupted by Frank's entrance, "and the NHS in general, is more concerned with ticking boxes, meeting targets and securing finance, than concentrating on the needs of the patients," she announced in a loud, strident voice.

"Some of that is certainly true," the young woman facing the group agreed. She was slim, her small oval face framed by long dark hair. Her eyes, large, dark, glistening pools, fastened on the woman with an unwavering gaze. "But the health service needs to function. Base as it is, money makes the world go around. The nursing staff continue to provide the best service they can with the resources available to them. Very few of the staff come into the NHS believing that it will make them millionaires."

"We don't blame the hospital staff," the woman who spoke had lank, bleached hair and tired looking eyes. Frank recognised her as Liam's mother. "He should never have been left in that flat on his own."

The young woman looked down at her lap. Probably unconsciously her right hand lifted and her fingers toyed with the small pendant suspended around her neck on a slim, silver chain. From her position Frank could not see the necklace clearly, but she knew what it was. She had seen it many times before. Attacked to the chain was a small silver angel, at its heart a tiny, light catching diamond.

.

"After care!" Liam's father, a squat, florid faced man with a bristling, grey moustache, said. "That's where everything falls apart."

"After care," Emily echoed and dropped her necklace. It fell against her cream, silk blouse. She looked across the room into Frank's eyes as she spoke. "I can assure you that is something we are particularly, and personally, dedicated to."

## Afterword.

The grey, anonymous people, the nurses, care assistants and associated staff who keep the NHS functioning are the real heroes of this story. They are not average people, they are extraordinary. They work long hours, often at the expense of their own health and personal lives, in spite of the machinations of managers and politicians, to provide care and treatment unequalled anywhere in the world.

In this story I have taken a step beyond that. I imagined where we would all end up, all of us who cared and worked to help other people. What our live would amount to.

I'm sure we won't end as ghosts tethered to our pasts and chained to crumbling asylums. But, equally surely, I know I'm not the only nurse who will enter retirement thinking about that one patient. That one who, perhaps with another word, or another action, would have taken a different course. With a different outcome.

Duty of care.

We're all haunted by the past.

**Kev Kirk 2018.**

Printed in Great Britain
by Amazon